# Strange Visitors

# Strange Visitors

## Eric Brown

Imaginings
An imprint of
NEWCON PRESS
NewCon Press
England

Eric Brown

One of a Special Edition, Signed by the Author
Limited to just 150 numbered copies
This is number:

112

Imaginings 1: Cold Grey Stones – Tanith Lee
Imaginings 2: Last and First Contacts – Stephen Baxter
Imaginings 3: Stories from the Northern Road – Tony Ballantyne
Imaginings 4: Objects in Dreams – Lisa Tuttle
Imaginings 5: Microcosmos – Nina Allan
Imaginings 6: Feast And Famine – Adrian Tchaikovsky
Imaginings 7: Twember – Steve Rasnic Tem
Imaginings 8: Strange Visitors – Eric Brown

I'd like to thank the following editors of the magazines and anthologies where these stories first appeared: Pete Crowther, Philip Harbottle, Mike Ashley, George Mann, Andy Remic, Lee Harris – and a big thanks too to Ian Whates.

First edition, published in the UK April 2014
by NewCon Press

IMG 008 hardback

10 9 8 7 6 5 4 3 2 1



ISBN: 978-1-907069-63-5 (hardback)

Cover art by Jim Burns
Cover design by Andy Bigwood

Minimal editorial interference by Ian Whates
Text layout by Storm Constantine

Printed in the UK by Berforts Information Press

# Contents

# Eric Brown: An Introduction

## Ian Whates

If you were to ask Rog Peyton – stalwart of the British SF community, recent Guest of Honour at Eastercon alongside Neil Gaiman, Tanith Lee, China Miéville, and Charles Stross, and former owner of the much-lamented Andromeda book shop in Birmingham – who our greatest living SF writer is, he wouldn't hesitate. "Eric Brown," he would tell you, with a conviction that brooks no argument.

The thing is, when somebody as respected as Rog makes an assertion like that, you have to pay attention. Could he be right?

I first met Eric at a convention several years ago and we hit it off immediately. That evening a group of us went out for a curry – Eric, Ian Watson, Tony Ballantyne, Mark Charan Newton and myself – and it was in the taxi on the way into Walsall that I learned of Eric's respect for the classic SF authors and his love for the writing of one in particular: Michael Coney. This will hardly come as a surprise to anyone familiar with Eric's work. The sensibilities of writers such as Coney and Clifford D. Simak suffuse every sentence, every scene. Yet Eric is no plagiarist, no literary leach; rather than attempting to recreate anyone's oeuvre, he never fails to establish and expand upon his own. He possesses a fertile imagination which guides his writing in myriad directions – classic in style, modern in execution, often crafting the type of tale that a Simak or a Coney might well have written were they with us today. Nor are his influences limited solely to genre fiction. Eric is widely read, as stories such as "Bukowski on Mars, with Beer" in this volume clearly demonstrate.

In 2009 I was fortunate enough to publish Eric's novella *Starship Fall*. This is a follow up to the wonderful *Starship Summer* and forms part of an eventual quartet of novellas set on Chalcedony that feature David Conway and his friends (readers may note certain parallels between Chalcedony and the Sapphire Oasis, setting for "The Sins of Edward Veron" here). I was thrilled when Eric offered me the second

Chalcedony piece, which contains all the elements I so enjoyed in the first. Principle among these is the cast of characters, whom I bought into within the first few pages.

Therein rests Eric's greatest attribute. While other writers attempt to dazzle a reader with technical expertise and scientific glitz, Eric chooses to highlight something far more fundamental: what it means deep down to be human. No matter how outlandish the setting or extravagant the trappings, at the heart of any Eric Brown story you will encounter a believable, fallible, sometimes noble and usually likeable, person. The story itself then evolves as we discover how such characters cope with extraordinary circumstance and unexpected events, creating drama that drives the narrative forward. No great secret. This is, after all, what many authors aspire to, but few manage it as successfully.

So, is Eric Brown our greatest living science fiction writer? Some may agree with this bold claim, while others may reject it entirely and still others may choose to qualify it by inserting the words 'one of'. The only way to form an opinion, of course, is to read his work; and where better to start than with a volume of original and previously uncollected stories?

Personally, I consider Eric Brown to be an outstanding writer whose work deserves to be cherished. Besides, who am I to argue with Rog Peyton?

*Ian Whates*
*Cambridgeshire*
*December 2013*

# Life Beyond...

*I've always enjoyed the stories and novels of Clifford D. Simak. He wrote from the '30s right through to the '80s, but he was at his best in the '50s and '60s. At the time when many of his US contemporaries were writing of aliens as a threat – this was at the height of the Cold War – Simak wrote quiet, humane tales of aliens as neighbours, down-home folk not dissimilar to you or me. Among his finest work are the novels Way Station, All Flesh is Grass, and A Choice of Gods. His short story about an alien and a farmer who helps him, the wonderful and moving "A Death in the House", is among my favourite tales by any writer.*

*"Life Beyond..." is my affectionate homage to the Grand Master.*

My house sits on the edge of the bluff with a fine sweeping view across the pine covered valley; from the big window in my study-cum-lounge I can see the distant Mississippi winding through the lush Wisconsin meadowland.

I was sitting on my old beat-up sofa – which Ellie my grand-daughter calls Feral on account of its looking wild. I was reading Thoreau and looking up from time to time and smiling to myself – that complicit smile acknowledging the privilege of being addressed by the dead, personally, through the depths of space and time.

The sun was setting on another hot summer's day and the sky was cloudless. You could see everything there was to see in that sky, distant birds and the contrails of the domestic jet-liners from O'Hare, and whatever else that might drop from the heavens, a-visiting.

On the sofa beside me was the small booklet that Ellie had written on her laptop. She had presented it to me after dinner, a little shyly, eyes downcast, before slipping off to bed. She had always said she wanted to be a writer, like me. I had assumed that it was another of her short stories, and wondered at her skittishness.

So I'd laid aside Thoreau and began reading Ellie's booklet, and soon *Excursions* was forgotten, and the impending visit of the interfering social worker too.

Oh, Ellie, Ellie... If words were the currency of our humanity, then my grand-daughter was rich beyond compare.

I wept.

The piece was entitled *My Life*, and began: *One month ago my Mom was killed in an automobile smash, and since then I've lived with Grampa in his big, old book-filled place on the hill, and I love Grampa more than anything in the world but I miss my Mom so much it's like a pain inside me...*

It went on, for over ten thousand words, describing her life before the accident, her life since, and the incomprehensible tragedy of her loss.

I finished reading the booklet, and then climbed the stairs and stood in the doorway of Ellie's room. She was asleep face down on the bed, still dressed: too-small tee-shirt and too-small jeans stretched tight on her spurting adolescent frame.

I was glad she was asleep: I could have offered only hugs and kisses and tears in consolation, in lieu of any explanation.

I returned to the lounge and considered the imminent meeting. I wanted to be sharp when the social worker came to try to take Ellie away from me.

She had called me earlier, a young woman with a posh Boston accent, ringing from a gas station off highway 94 to apologize. She was running late; my place was hard to find; she'd miscalculated how much gasoline she would need.

I found myself reassuring her, friendly-like, telling her not to worry: this stranger out to wreck my life.

She'd said she would find a motel for the night and see me in the morning, but I assured her that tonight would be fine. I wanted to get the meeting over and done with.

Now I heard movement above my head. Evidently Ellie had awoken. I heard the window of her room swing open and the window-seat creak. No doubt she was hugging her knees, staring out at the night and the stars, as she had made it her habit to do over the weeks.

I smiled and continued reading.

Minutes later there was all-hell of a din as Ellie jumped from the window-seat and thumped across the bare boards and raced down the stairs and arrived, breathless, in the doorway to the lounge, gasping at me.

"What's spooking you, girl?" I said, amused.

"Gramps! Look! Look in the sky over Wilson's forest! I saw it coming down from way up! There, see it?"

She ran into the room and vaulted over the back of the sofa, landing beside me and hugging me to her, pointing through the window.

It took some while for my old eyes to adjust, then I saw what had excited her so.

It was a silver thing, all twinkling and scintillating in the light of the setting sun. Hard to tell how big it was – maybe the size of a light aircraft – but it was stubby, torpedo-shaped and wingless, and was angling down steeply over the treetops. I caught a five second glimpse of Ellie's mysterious object before it dropped into the forest and vanished.

We looked at each other. My grand-daughter's eyes were wide.

"What was it, Gramps?"

Common-sense took hold of me. "Either a bit of some old satellite, El, or a weather balloon, most like."

"Bor-ing! Not a UFO or a time-machine?"

"You've got a lively imagination!"

She glanced at her booklet, then at my book. "What you reading, Gramps?"

"Thoreau."

"Did you read...?"

I pulled her to me and kissed her mussed-up blonde curls. She was eleven years old and gawky, with nascent beauty in the lineaments of her face, just waiting to explode. I could see a lot of Sam, my daughter, in her.

"We'll talk in the morning," I said. "Now off to bed, and sleep, okay?"

She gave me another tight squeeze, then slipped from the sofa and hurried back upstairs.

I might have let her stay up a while, and talked to her some, but I had seen, way away on the winding track that led to my house and nowhere else, the beetling shape of a Buick.

I poured myself a stiff bourbon; I wanted to have my wits about me when I faced Miss-whatever-her-name-was, but also I wanted something to take the edge off my anger.

Five minutes later the Buick rounded the last bend and drew to a halt. The driver climbed from the car and walked the rest of the way up the pot-holed track, pausing to peer at the house with a hand fitted to her brow.

She was tall and smartly dressed, with long dark hair and a strong, intelligent, city-wise face.

She was carrying something, as well as her valise. I hoped it wasn't what I thought it was.

I left the lounge and hauled open the front door before she had time to ring the chime.

"Mr Robertshaw, I'm so sorry."

"Call me Ed. Don't worry, I keep elastic hours." It wasn't what I had meant to say, but I always find it hard to cold-shoulder folk, even social workers.

"I'm Elizabeth Kovac. We spoke at length last week."

And she *was* clutching, in her beautifully-manicured right hand, what I'd feared. I winced as I led her through the house to the lounge.

She sat in an armchair and I collapsed into the sofa.

"Mr Robertshaw, Ed – it's a pleasure to meet you."

"I only wish the circumstances were a little more conducive to bonhomie," I said.

I could see her glancing around the room, at the disorderly piles of books, then at my somewhat disheveled appearance.

I was not what she was expecting a grand old man of letters to be.

She placed my latest novel on the arm of the chair and patted it, somewhat primly.

"Ed, I've been reading your books for years. I can't tell you how much I enjoy them."

I shrugged. I always find praise embarrassing.

"I was wondering if you might sign it?"

I hesitated, then dragged it to me and found a pen. I scribbled my name and closed the book.

Her glance alighted on the ream of quarto on my desk. Her eyes widened. "Your latest?"

I refrained from saying, "And probably my last." I'd finished the third draft of what I considered my finest novel shortly before my daughter's death, and the accident had knocked me sideways and pushed from my mind all thoughts of ever writing again.

"I take it you and your team read my letter and the adoption papers," I said.

She sighed. "Mr Robertshaw – Ed. As I said on the phone, this is an exceptional case, and in any other circumstance we might have considered your application."

"Ellie's happy here," I said, despising myself for the note of desperation in my voice. "She wants to stay with me."

"To be perfectly frank, Ed, the child's desire in cases like this is not our paramount concern."

"Then what is?"

"The long-term welfare of your grand-daughter."

"I too have that in mind."

She looked at me. She said, pointedly, "The *long-term* welfare, Ed?"

*Touché.*

"I'm as fit and healthy now as I was at the age of forty," I blustered.

She smiled. "How old are you, Ed?"

I stared at her. She was, I guessed, around thirty, a mere child.

"Seventy-five last fall," I said.

She was smiling at me, patronizing. She no longer saw me as the patriarchal novelist; now I was some crusty backwoods hermit bordering on senility.

"Ed, please try to see the situation from my point of view. Ellie needs care for the next six, seven years. With all due respect, you might not be able to provide that care."

"I don't want El in a home," I said.

"Let me assure you that Ellie will be fostered by a caring family short-term, while a suitable long-term adoptive family is located."

"But my grand-daughter is happy with me!" I began.

She leafed through some papers and then looked up at me. "Ed, I discovered that last fall you suffered a minor coronary."

I stared at her, gestured helplessly. "Minor..." I echoed.

"You didn't inform us."

"Didn't think it mattered that much," I said.

Kovac became business-like. "Ed, we'll do everything within our powers to keep Ellie nearby. We recognize the mutual need for continued contact..." Kovac went on, but she was spouting text-book stuff at me now, and I turned off.

I thought through the best way to tell Kovac that I wasn't giving in – that I wouldn't give up Ellie without a fight.

From her valise she withdrew a sheaf of forms and laid them on the coffee table between us. "If you could complete the relevant details and get them back to me..."

"And if I refuse?"

"Ed, that wouldn't be advisable. We'd have to take the matter to court, and that would only prolong the entire procedure."

"And I'd have Ellie for a little bit longer."

She stared at me. She clearly thought me an old fool – which I probably was. "Ed, Ellie would be taken from you and placed in a care home for the duration of the litigation. It would only prove even more upsetting for her."

I gave her my fiercest stare. "So in effect what you're saying is that I have no say in the matter? Even though I love my grand-daughter and want her to stay, and Ellie wants to stay too, there's absolutely no way you're going to listen to what *we* want?"

"Ed, as I've tried to explain, we have the best interests of Ellie in mind. If only you could see that."

We bickered back and forth for a time, getting nowhere. I succeeded only in increasing my blood pressure some.

At last I stood and indicated the door. "I think we each know where the other stands on the matter," I said in my most formal and pompous manner.

She rose to leave. "I was hoping that this could be settled amicably," she began.

I saw her to the door – almost tossing her copy of my novel after her – and watched her drive away down the track and out of sight.

I made my way up to El's room and stood in the doorway. She was asleep, under the sheets this time, her clothes folded neatly at the foot of the bed.

I stood there for perhaps fifteen minutes, my head full of images of Ellie as a baby, a toddler, a feisty, independent nine year-old...

I was seventy-five, but I was good for another ten years. I would fight Kovac and the system with every means available to me. Maybe I was an old fool, but since Sam's death Ellie had become more precious to me than anything else.

She was my life.

I made my way downstairs and, almost without realizing what I was doing, I picked up the bottle of bourbon, took a long swallow and stared out through the window.

I had told Ellie that the thing had been an old satellite, or a weather balloon...

Perhaps, looking back, I was drawn to leave the house. Or perhaps it never happened. Perhaps my memory of the following events is false, the result of too much alcohol on top of so much pent-up anger.

Whatever, I recall leaving the house and making my way along the track toward Wilson's forest.

I was still clutching the bottle of bourbon.

It was that time of night when coons are abroad, moving cautiously through the undergrowth, and the first owls are tuning up. A full moon climbed high above the pines, and the last of the sunlight was reddening like a hemorrhage in the west.

I was *drawn*. Looking back, that's how it seems. I was an old fool to be out with a bottle of bourbon and my regrets when the sun was almost down, but it didn't seem that way.

The night air was resinous, and I recall the sense of excitement, apropos of nothing, as I left the track and took the footpath toward the forest.

I climbed through the pines, the twilight suddenly deepening, and out of the last light of the sun a sudden chill came upon me. I think I even stopped and wondered why I'd left Ellie all alone back there – not that she was in any danger, being that the nearest human habitation was nigh on twenty-five miles away.

I pressed on. I stopped once to take a chug of bourbon and then continued my climbing. I was heading toward where I judged the *thing* had come down, though quite how I might have judged that I do not know.

Then I saw a glint of silver through the trees and increased my pace.

Whatever this was, it had shaved down a good dozen sturdy pines on its entry into the forest. Now the object stood on the edge of a bluff, its nose projecting out over the edge, with a fan-tail of pulverized matchwood in its wake.

I stopped dead in my tracks, and pushed my hand through my

thinning hair; I might even have said *God-dang-it.*

In front of me was a blunt torpedo, perhaps twenty feet long, and silver. At its nose was a wrap-around viewscreen kind of thing, and halfway down its length a cartoon mousehole-shaped opening.

A short ramp led down from the opening.

I don't mind allowing that I took a good few swallows of bourbon at the sight.

I stepped forward and approached the craft. Courage had nothing to do with my advance; like I said, I was drawn.

The vessel's occupant had taken advantage of a fallen log and was admiring the view beyond the drop. Half the county was bathed in the light of the sun, all faded green and hazy gold.

The creature was humanoid and very thin, almost skeletal, with very white skin, the regulation number of eyes, a nose and a mouth; but its features were curiously flattened and expressionless. I gained the impression that it was male, though of course in that I might have been mistaken.

It wore a little gray suit consisting of knee-length trousers and a short-sleeved shirt.

"You live," it said, "in a beautiful part of the world."

I nodded. "I like to think so."

"I think it's important to take the time to appreciate natural beauty," it went on.

"There is nothing like," I said, "Wisconsin at sundown in summer."

The being gestured to the log. "Won't you join me?"

You think it strange, I guess, that I am so matter of fact in reporting the first recorded instance of human contact with an extraterrestrial. In my defense let me state that although a part of me was aware of the significance of the event, it was as if my intellect had been tranquilized. I am sure that the alien was responsible for this, and not the bourbon.

Perhaps, without its feat of telepathic tranquilization, I might have been a gibbering wreck.

I sat down on the log next to the creature.

I found myself saying, "You have come a long way?"

Of all the questions to ask a traveler from the stars!

"Since my last stop," it said, "not that far. A matter of a hundred light years or so."

"Is that all?" I nodded. "And before that?"

"I have travelled through the inhabited system for almost fifty of your years," it said. "Some hundred thousand light years."

Now let me say that, although it communicated to me in good old American English, its words were not synchronized to the movement of its lips, and the effect was similar to that of watching a badly dubbed foreign film.

I fidgeted. My old bones were a little uncomfortable without a back-rest. I sat down on the mossy floor of the clearing and lodged my back against the log.

My alien companion did likewise.

"A good idea," it said.

I took a swallow of bourbon and, remembering my manners, offered the bottle to my guest.

It regarded the bottle. "Go on," I said. "We call this bourbon. Has quite a kick. Try it."

With seeming caution it reached out, took the bottle, and raised it experimentally to its lips. A good tumblerful of alcohol slid down its long gullet, without ill-effect.

It returned the bottle. "Interesting."

I gestured to the ship beside us. "Quite a vessel you have yourself there."

"You would think, wouldn't you, that after fifty years of star travel I would have perfected the landing manoeuvre?"

I shrugged, not knowing much about that line of thing.

"I feared my ship would be damaged, but after a thorough inspection I am happy to report that it needs but minor repairs."

"That's good to hear." I hesitated. "Perhaps I might be able to help."

"That's very kind of you, but it won't take me long."

I nodded. "And then you'll be on your way?"

"I will, though I had hoped to have time to do what I came to this planet to do."

I took another swig of bourbon, and passed the bottle. My friend drank too. For an alien, it liked its liquor.

"And what," I asked, "did you come to Earth to do?"

I can hear you asking: the annihilation of the entire human race?

The reconnaissance of all military establishments preparatory to an alien invasion?

I thought nothing of the sort. I kind of trusted the alien by then. But I was curious.

"I make it my duty," it said, "to collect on every planet I visit an example of its literature. In short, I collect books."

I stared at the critter beside me. I hadn't taken it for a bookworm.

"Books?" I said. "I mean, other planets possess books? I thought maybe Earth was unique in having them. I would have thought that other planets had... well, other means of... of recording things." I realized I was babbling and shut up.

Listen to me! Other planets? Until that time I hadn't given much thought to the possibility that other, inhabited worlds might have existed beyond planet Earth.

"Oh, all sentient races the galaxy over have had, at some point in their history, objects known as books in one form or another."

"And you collect them?" I asked.

He turned his bland, flat face to me and essayed, for the first time, a smile. It failed to work fully – the effect resembled a stretched elastic band – but I appreciated the effort.

"I pick up three items from every planet I visit."

"Only three?"

"Inhabited planets are multifarious, and my ship is only small."

"And when you return to your homeworld, will you sell these books?"

"I am not a businessman," it said. "I donate the books to the Library of Lithia. My planet stands at a junction in the spaceway. Many races come to Lithia to study at the Library."

I stared in open-mouthed wonder at my informant.

I recalled what it had said, earlier. "But you fear that you don't have enough time to collect your quota of books?"

The alien stared out over the bluff, into the deepening night. I honestly think that it was quite taken with the landscape.

"That is so. The repair will take a little while. Then I will have to depart. I am expected back at Lithia in one month, Earth-time."

Something like vast melancholy opened up inside me. I thought of the Library of Lithia, and the fact that it would be without any examples of human books.

Impulsively I asked, "How long will your repairs take?"

"Perhaps one of your hours," it replied.

"In that case," I said, scrambling to my feet, "I'll bring you three books before you leave. For the Library. A present from the people of Earth!" I stopped and stared at the alien, who was looking up at me with large eyes. Did I see gratitude in those great milky orbs, or was that wishful thinking on my part? "But which three books?" I asked.

"Allow your heart to make that choice," said the alien. "But I will state that I require books which reflect what it is to be a human being, books written with emotion, and not text books or scientific treatises."

I nodded. "I'll return within the hour with three suitable volumes," I promised.

The alien stood also and, briefly halting my progress from the clearing, said, "And I will give you something in return, Ed."

"You will?" I said, and hurried from the clearing. It was not until I was well down the incline, the starship hidden from view, that I wondered how the alien had known my name.

I made my way home at a shambling jog, having to stop from time to time to ease my ageing legs and lungs. Only when the house came into sight, lighted against the darkness that loomed behind the bluff, did I realize what a responsibility the alien had charged me with: my imminent choice would dictate to countless alien scholars their knowledge and understanding of planet Earth...

I rushed into the house and stood in the middle of my study, surrounded by shelves of books from floor to ceiling, books piled tottering on the floor, books spilling from chairs and boxes; thousands of books, millions, perhaps billions, of words; the concentrated thoughts of legion of thinkers from humankind's vast history...

And my alien friend wanted me to choose just three!

I paced my study. I pulled down volume after volume, made a primary pile, and a secondary pile, keeping the alien's dicta uppermost in my mind. Books written with emotion, which told what it was to be human...

When I looked up I saw that almost an hour had elapsed, and I panicked. What if they alien had departed in his silver starship without three human books for Lithia?

Minutes later I was near to making my choice.

The complete worlds of Shakespeare, of course.

The Bible... or the Koran, the Talmud, the Bardo Thodol, the Bhagavad-Gita?

I looked across the room, and saw upon the desk the manuscript of my latest novel, the novel which I thought summed up so many years of fictive endeavor.

If I were to slip it into a binder, present it to the alien as the third book...

To think of it, my words read by creatures from far stars!

Then my gaze fell on the booklet Ellie had given me earlier that evening.

Trembling, I crossed the room and picked up her heartfelt outpouring of loss and love and hope.

In my other hand I hefted my weighty manuscript, and then, after careful consideration, laid it aside.

I carried Ellie's *My Life* back to the pile I had made on the floor, selected two further books and hurried from the house.

My heart was thudding with the knowledge of the choice I had made, and the thought of these three volumes residing in the distant stellar library. What a gift to the stars – what an honor for the human race!

I turned from the track and took the path into the pines. I climbed, my heartbeat banging. I searched desperately for the glimpse of silver between the trees, insane with the thought that the alien had departed already – or that I had hallucinated the entire meeting.

But there it was.

I stumbled, exhausted, into the clearing and approached the starship.

The alien emerged from the opening within the ship's flank and came down the ramp toward me.

The alien paused, and again that strange smile played upon its unpractised lips as I held out the books.

It took them from me one by one.

"This one?" it asked, and I explained that this was a revered holy book.

"And this?"

I gave a brief synopsis, hardly doing justice to the author's genius.

"And the third?" it asked.

"This," I said, my voice trembling, "this is the true account of a young girl's grief at losing the person she loved the most, but it is also a... a testament to the power of hope for the future that lives in the heart of every human being."

The alien tucked the three books under its arm.

"The only thing I can give you in return, Ed," said the alien being, "is advice."

"Advice?" I echoed.

"Sometimes we must relinquish that which we treasure the most, Ed. You see," it went on, before I could say a word, "I have learned this from experience. For many of your years I have garnered from around the galaxy the most fabulous items from the most fabulous planets. I refer to books, of course. Then, on my way back to Lithia, a device I have aboard the ship translates the books into my own language, and I have time to read them, and the many wonders they contain – and by the time of my arrival I have grown fond of the books in my possession, so fond that I am loathe to give them up to the library."

"But you do?" I said.

It smiled. "I do. Books need to be read in order to grow, Ed. I could not selfishly keep them for myself. They belong in the world beyond."

And, before I could move or say another word, with its free hand the alien reached out to me.

"One must accept, Ed."

It touched my face, in a gesture I might have found disconcerting had it been made by another man. But his touch, on my cheek, filled me with peace and joy – and acceptance.

I backed away, toward the edge of the clearing, as the alien climbed the ramp into its ship.

At the top, the creature turned and lifted a hand in parting.

The opening vanished, and seconds later the starship lifted without a sound and moved slowly out over the bluff. It accelerated into the night sky and in an instant was lost among the stars.

I stared up at the massed constellations, my head filled with the wonder of far stars, and alien cities and civilizations. Then I made my slow way home to where a young girl, at the very start of her life, was sleeping the sleep of the innocent, and maybe dreaming.

And as I went it came to me what a pig-headed, cussed, ornery old fool I'd been.

Back home, I climbed the stairs and stood by Ellie's bedroom door for a long time, wondering how to tell her that, for her own good, she would have to leave me.

All that happened ten years ago, and I survived. I even wrote more novels, inspired perhaps by my memory of the alien.

Ellie left and lived with kind adoptive parents over Millville way, and I do believe they were the very best thing for her. A professor and his librarian wife, they broadened her mind in a way I doubt I could have done.

I visited Ellie every month – but I never told her of my strange encounter with the bibliophile alien that night.

She is sleeping in her old bed above my head as I write this, returned from university for the summer break. Tomorrow is her twenty-first birthday. I have never been back to the clearing in Wilson's forest, perhaps fearing that there will be no evidence to corroborate my memories...

And the gaps in my shelves, from where I took the books? And the fact that, on the morning after Ellie gave me her booklet, it was nowhere to be found in the house?

Tomorrow, after breakfast, as a birthday present, I will take my grand-daughter over to Wilson's forest. I will tell her of that miraculous night ten years ago, the night she saw the starship fall to Earth; I will show her the trees scattered like jackstraws, and tell her that she is the author of a work read by all manner of alien beings across the vast expanse of the galaxy, a work of pain, and grief – and of boundless love and hope rewarded.

# Steps Along the Way

*I don't write many post human stories – I just don't get many ideas that fit into the sub-genre. I tend to write relatively near-future tales, or about futures not too dissimilar to our own. Critics might call me a dinosaur, and they'd have a case – what with the fast-approaching singularity, after which everything will be different... But I must admit that I find many post-human stories dissatisfying on a humane, emotional level: we all like to read tales where we can relate to the central characters, right, and how can we do that if the human protagonists are changed out of all recognition? Anyway, here's my take on the post-human tale, done with a modicum of emotion.*

On the eve of my five hundredth rebirthday, as I strolled the gardens of my manse, a messenger appeared and informed me that I had a visitor.

"Severnius wishes to consult you on a matter of urgency," said the ball of light. "Shall I make an appointment?"

"Severnius? How long has it been? No – I'll see him now."

The light disappeared.

It was the end of a long Autumn afternoon, and a low sun filled the garden with a rich and hazy light. I had been contemplating my immediate future, quite how I should approach the next century. I am a man methodical and naturally circumspect: not for me the grand announcements of intent detailing how I might spend my *next* five hundred years. I prefer to plan ahead one hundred years at a time, ever hopeful of the possibility of change, within myself and without. For the past week I had considered many avenues of enquiry and pursuit; but none had appealed. I had awoken early that morning, struck with an idea like a revelation: Quietus.

I composed myself on a marble bench beneath an arbour entwined with fragrant roses. The swollen sun sank amid bright tangerine strata, and on the other side of the sky the moon rose, full yet insubstantial, above the manse.

Severnius stepped from the converter and crossed the glade. He always wore his primary soma-form when we met, as a gesture of respect: that of a wise-man of yore, with flowing silver-grey hair and beard. He was a Fellow some two thousand years old, garbed in the magenta robes of the Academy.

We embraced in silence, a short communion in which I reacquainted myself with his humanity.

"Fifty years?" I asked.

He smiled. "More like eighty," he said, and then gave the customary greeting of these times: "To your knowledge."

"Your knowledge," I responded.

We sat and I gestured, and wine and glasses appeared upon the bench between us.

"Let me see, the last time we met you were still researching the Consensus of Rao."

"I concluded that it was an unworkable proposition, superseded by the latest theories." I smiled. "But worth the investigation."

Severnius sipped his wine. "And now?"

"I wound down my investigations ten years ago, and since then I've been exploring the Out-there. Seeking the new..."

He smiled, something almost condescending in his expression. He was my patron and teacher; he was disdainful of the concept of the new.

"Where are you now?" he asked. "What have you found?"

"Much as ever, permutations of what has been and what is known." I closed my eyes, and made contact. "$I^2$ is on Pharia, in the Nilakantha Stardrift, taking in the ways of the natives there; $I^3$ is climbing Selerious Mons on Titan, and $I^4$ is in love with a quasi-human on a nameless moon half a galaxy away."

"It appears that you are... *waiting*?" he said. "Biding your time with meaningless pursuits. Considering your options for the next century."

I hesitated. It occurred to me then how propitious was his arrival. I would never have gone ahead with Quietus without consulting him.

"A thought came to me this morning, Severnius. Five hundred years is a long time. With your tutelage and my enquiries..." I gestured, "I have learned much, dare I say everything? I was contemplating a period of Quietus."

He nodded, considering my words. "A possibility," he agreed. "Might I enquire as to the duration?"

"It really only occurred to me at dawn. I don't know – perhaps a thousand years."

"I once enjoyed Quietus for five hundred," said Severnius. "I was reinvigorated upon awakening – the thrill of change, the knowledge of all the learning to be caught up with."

"Precisely my thoughts."

"There is an alternative, of course."

I stared at him. "There is?"

He hesitated, marshalling his words. "My Fellows at the Academy last week Enstated and Enabled an Early," he said. "The process, though wholly successful physiologically, was far from psychologically fulfilled. We had to wipe his memories of the initial awakening and instruction. We are ready to try again."

I stared at him. The Enstating and Enabling of an Early was a rare occurrence indeed. I said as much.

"You," Severnius said, "were the last."

Even though I had been considered a success, my rehabilitation had required his prolonged patronage. I thought through what he had told me so far, the 'urgency' of his presence here.

He was smiling. "I have been watching your progress closely these past eighty years," he said. "I submitted your name to the Academy. We agreed that you should be made a Fellow, subject to the successful completion of a certain test."

"And that is?" I asked, aware of my heartbeat. All thought of Quietus fled at the prospect of becoming a Fellow.

"The patronage and stewardship of the Early we Enstated and Enabled last week," Severnius said.

It was a while before I could bring myself to reply. It was a great honour to be considered by the Academy, but at the same time I fully understood the difficulties of patronage. "You said that the subject was psychologically damaged."

Severnius gestured. "You studied advanced psycho-healing in your second century. We have confidence in your abilities."

"It will be a considerable undertaking. A hundred years, more?"

"When we Enstated and Enabled you, I was your steward for almost fifty years. We think that perhaps a hundred years might suffice in this case."

"Perhaps," I said, "before I make a decision I might meet the subject?"

Severnius nodded. "By all means," he said, and while he gave me the details of the Early, his history, I closed my eyes and made contact. I recalled $I^2$ from his studies on Pharia, $I^3$ from Titan, and $I^4$ from his affair with the alien.

Minutes later $I^2$, $I^3$, and $I^4$ followed each other from the converter and stepped across the glade, calling greetings to Severnius. They appeared as younger, carefree versions of myself, before age and wisdom had cured me of vanity. I stood and reached out, and we merged.

Their thoughts, their respective experiences on Pharia, Titan and the nameless moon, became mine – and while they had revelled in their experiences, to me they were the antics of children, and I learned nothing new. I resolved to edit the memories when an opportune moment arose.

Severnius, with the etiquette of the time, had averted his gaze during the process of merging. Now he looked up and smiled. "You are ready?"

I stood. We crossed to the converter, and then, before stepping upon the plate, both paused to look up at our destination.

The moon, riding higher now, and more substantial against the darker sky, gazed down on us with a face altered little since time immemorial. The fact of its immutability, in an age passé with the boundless possibilities of change, filled me with awe.

We converted.

The Halls of the Fellowship of the Academy occupied the Sea of Tranquillity, an agglomeration of domes scintillating in the sunlight against the absolute black of the Lunar night.

We stepped from the converter and crossed the regolith towards the Academy. Severnius led me into the cool, hushed shade of the domes and through the hallowed halls. He explained that if I agreed to steward the Early, then the ceremony of acceptance to the Fellowship would follow immediately. I glanced at him. He clearly assumed that I would accept without question.

The idea of ministering to the psychological well-being of an Early, for an indefinite duration, filled me with apprehension.

We came to the interior dome. The sight of the subject within the silver hemisphere, trapped like some insect for inspection, brought forth in me a rush of memories and emotions. Five hundred years ago I too had awoken to find myself within a similar dome. Five hundred years ago, I presume, I had looked just as frightened and bewildered as this Early.

A gathering of Fellows – Academics, Scientists, Philosophers – stood in a semi-circle around the dome, watching with interest and occasionally addressing comments to their colleagues. Upon the arrival of Severnius and myself, they made discreet gestures of acknowledgement and departed, some vanishing within their own converters, others choosing to walk.

I approached the skin of the dome and stared.

The Early was seated upon the edge of a low foam-form, his elbows lodged upon his knees, his head in his hands. From time to time he looked up and stared about him, his clasped hands a knotted symbol of the fear in his eyes.

I felt an immediate empathy, a kinship.

Severnius had told me that he had died at the age of eighty-two, but they had restored him to a soma-type approximately half that age. His physique was lean and well-muscled, but his most striking attribute was his eyes, piercingly blue and intelligent.

I glanced at Severnius, who nodded. I walked around the dome, so that I would be facing the Early when I entered, and stepped through the skin of the hemisphere. Even then, my sudden arrival startled him. He looked up, his hands gripping his knees, and the fear in his eyes intensified.

He spoke, but in an accented English so primitive that it was some seconds before I could understand his words.

"Who the hell are you?" he said. "What's happening to me?"

I held up a reassuring hand and emitted pheromones to calm his nerves. In his own tongue I said, "Please, do not be afraid. I am a friend."

Despite the pheromones and my reassurances, he was still nervous. He stood quickly and stared at me. "What the hell's going on here?"

His agitation brought back memories. I recalled my own awakening, my first meeting with Severnius. He had seemed a hostile figure then. Humankind had changed over the course of thirty thousand years, become taller and more considerate in the expenditure of motion. He had appeared to me like some impossibly calm, other-worldly creature.

As I must have appeared to this Early.

"Please," I said, "sit down."

He did so, and I sat beside him, a hand on his arm. The touch eased him slightly.

"I'd like to know what's happening," he said, fixing me with his intense, sapphire stare. "I know this sounds crazy, but the last I remember... I was dying. I'd been ill for a while, and then the hospitalisation..."

He shook his head, tears appearing in his eyes as he gazed at his hands – the hands of a man half the age of the person he had been. I reached out and touched his arm, calming him.

"And then I woke up here, in this body. Hell, you don't know what it's like, to inhabit the body of an old man, and then to wake up suddenly... suddenly *young* again."

I smiled. I said nothing, but I could well recall the feeling, the wonder, the disbelief; the doubt and then the joy of apprehending the reality of renewal.

He looked up at me, quickly, something very much like terror in his eyes. "I'm alive, aren't I? This isn't some dream?"

"I assure you that what you are experiencing is no dream."

"So this is... Afterlife?"

"You could say that," I ventured. "Certainly, for you, this is an Afterlife." I emitted pheromones strong enough to forestall his disbelief.

He merely shook his head. "Where am I?" he asked in little more than a whisper.

"The time is more than thirty thousand years after the century of your birth."

"Thirty thousand years?" He enunciated each word separately, slowly.

"To you it might seem like a miracle beyond comprehension," I said, "but the very fact that you are here implies that the science of this age can accomplish what in your time would be considered magic. Imagine the reaction of a stone age man, say, to the wonders of twentieth century space flight."

He looked at me. "So... to you I'm nothing more than a primitive."

"Not at all," I said. "We deem you capable of understanding the concepts behind our world, though it might take a little time." This was a lie – there were many things that would be beyond his grasp for many years, even decades.

Severnius had told me that the subject had evinced signs of mental distress upon learning the disparity between his ability to understand and the facts as they were presented. I would have to be very careful with this subject – if, that was, I accepted the Fellowship.

"So," he said, staring at me. "Answer my question. How did you bring me here?"

"Very well..." I proceeded to explain, in terms he might understand, the scientific miracle of Enstating and Enabling. It was a ludicrously simplistic description of a complex process, of course, but it would suffice.

His eyes bored into me. His left cheek had developed a quick, nervous tic. "I don't believe it."

I touched his arm, the contact calming him. "Please... Why would I lie?"

"But how could you possibly recover my memories, my feelings?"

"Think of your childhood," I said, "your earliest memories. Think of your greatest joy, your greatest fear. Tell me, have we succeeded?"

His expression was anguished. "Christ," he whispered. "I can remember everything... everything. My childhood, college." He shook his head in slow amazement. "But... but my understanding of the way the universe works... it tells me this can't be happening."

I laughed. "Come! You are a man of science, a rationalist. Things change: what was taken as written in stone is overturned; theory gives way to established fact, which in turn evolves yet more fundamental theory, which is then verified... and so proceeds the advance of scientific enlightenment."

"I understand what you're saying," he said. "It's just that I'm finding it hard to believe."

"In time," I said, "you will come to accept the seeming miracles of this age."

Without warning he stood and strode towards the concave skin of the dome. He stared at his reflection, and then turned to face me.

"In time, you say? Just how long have I got?" He lifted his hand and stared at it. "Am I some laboratory animal you'll get rid of once your experiment's through?" He stopped and considered something. "If you built this body, then you must be able to keep it indefinitely..."

He stopped again, this time at something in my expression. I nodded. "You are immortal," I said.

I could see that he was shaken. The tight skin of his face coloured as he nodded, trying to come to terms with my casual pronouncement of his new status.

"Thirty thousand years in the future," he whispered to himself, "the world is inhabited by immortals."

"The galaxy," I corrected him. "Humankind has spread throughout the stars, inhabiting those planets amenable to life, adapting others, sharing worlds with intelligent beings."

Tears welled in his eyes. He fought not to let them spill, typical masculine product of the twentieth century that he was.

"If you did this for me," he said, "then it's within your capability to bring back to life the people I loved, my wife and family –"

"And where would we stop?" I asked. "Would we Enstate and Enable the loved ones of everyone we brought forward?" I smiled. "Where would it end? Soon, everyone who had ever lived would live again."

He failed to see the humour of my words. "You don't know how cruel that is," he said.

"I understand how cruel it seems," I said. "But it is the cruelty of necessity." I paused. I judged that the time was right to share my secret. "You see, I too was once like you, plucked from my death-bed, brought forward to this strange and wondrous age, fearful and little comprehending the miracles around me. I stand before you as testament to the fact that you will survive this ordeal, and come to understand."

He stared at me, suspicious. At last he said, "But why? Why you and me?"

"They, the people of this age, considered us men of importance in our time – men whose contribution to history were steps along the way to the position or pre-eminence that humankind now occupies. Ours is not to wonder, but to accept."

"So that's all I am – a curiosity? A specimen in some damned museum?"

"Not at all! They will be curious, of course; they'll want to hear all about your time... but you are free to learn, to explore, to do with your limitless future what you will – with the guidance and stewardship of a patron, as I too was once guided."

The Early walked around the periphery of the dome. He completed a circuit, and then halted and stared at me. "Explore," he said at last, tasting the word. "You said explore? I want to explore the worlds beyond Earth! No – not only the worlds beyond Earth, the worlds *beyond* the worlds you've already explored. I want to break new ground, discover new worlds..." He stopped and looked at me. "I take it that you haven't charted *all* the universe?"

I hesitated. "There are places still beyond the known expanses of space," I said.

"Then I want to go there!"

I smiled, taken by his naïve enthusiasm. "There will be time enough for exploration," I said. "First, you must be copied, so that you can send your other selves out to explore the unexplored. There are dangers –"

He was staring at me in disbelief, but his disbelief was not for what I thought. "Dangers?" he almost scoffed. "What's the merit of exploration if there's no risk?"

I opened my mouth, but this time I had no answer. Something of his primitivism, his heedless, reckless thirst for life which discounted peril and hardship, reminded me of the person I had once been, an age ago.

I considered the next one hundred years, and beyond. I had reached that time of my life when all experience seemed jejune and passé; I had come to the point, after all, where I had even considered Quietus.

To go beyond the uncharted, to endanger oneself in the quest for knowledge, to think the unthinkable...

It was ridiculous – but why, then, did the notion bring tears to my eyes?

I hurried across the dome and took his arm. "Come," I said, leading him towards the skin of the hemisphere.

"Where…?" he began.

But we were already outside the dome, and then through the skin of another, and walking across the silver-grey regolith of the lunar surface.

He stopped and gazed about him in wonder. "Christ," he whispered. "Oh, Christ, I never thought..."

"Over here," I said, leading him.

We crossed the plain towards the display, unchanged in thirty thousand years. He stared at the lunar module, stark beneath the unremitting light of the sun. We stood on the platform encircling the display and stared down at the footprints the first astronauts had laid upon the surface of another world.

He looked at me, his expression beatific. "I often dreamed," he said, "but I never thought I'd ever return."

I smiled. I shared the emotions he experienced, then. I knew what it was to return. I recalled the time, not long after my rebirth in this miraculous age, when I had made the pilgrimage to Earth and looked again upon the cell where over thirty thousand years ago I, Galileo Galilei, had been imprisoned for my beliefs.

Haltingly, I told Armstrong who I was. We stared up into the dark sky, past the Earth and the brilliant sun, to the wonders awaiting us in the uncharted universe beyond.

We embraced for a long minute, and then turned and retraced our steps across the surface of the moon towards the domes of the Academy, where Severnius would be awaiting my decision.

# The Sins of Edward Veron

*Here's another story – like the first – in which a visitor from the stars brings about change to the life of the human being he meets. (It's a theme I've returned to from time to time: there are other tales later in this volume along similar lines). This one is set in my artists resort of Sapphire Oasis, a venue I've used for a number of stories. It also features an artist haunted by past deeds, a new art form, and apotheosis – all things I've written about before, in various ways.*

Around seven, as the sun set and brought about another quick Saharan twilight, I realised that I had done all I could do to the crystal that day. I pulled off the glove, ripped the wires from my head and stared at the incomplete, crystalline fragment with something close to despair.

I reached out, ran my hands over the faceted surface and felt anger and jealousy and guilt. An outsider experiencing these emotions in the crystal might have thought them genuine, even profound. To myself, who knew what I wanted to achieve, the work seemed forced and shallow.

I looked up, through the clear membrane of my dome, and was surprised to see that night had fallen. A panoply of bright stars filled the heavens, reminding me of that evening's big event.

The arrival of the extraterrestrial.

I decided to watch the event from the balcony of my studio. I set myself up with a few beers and sat in the balmy night. Down below, around the oasis, a crowd of fellow artists had gathered. They sipped cocktails and chatted amongst themselves, but with that terrible self-consciousness I have noticed amongst minor celebrities who have one eye constantly on the look-out for bigger names to snare.

All week the conversation in Sapphire Oasis had been about the arrival of the alien from Mintaka V. What kind of art might the alien produce? Why had it selected Sapphire Oasis, among the many other artist colonies on Earth, in which to produce its work?

I had been as intrigued as my colleagues. Mintaka had seven planets, the fifth of which was inhabited. Felekka was the name of the planet, and the aliens were humanoid air-breathers, sufficiently like human beings to allow easy contact between the species.

I had seen pix of the Felekkans on vids and in books: small, pale green beings, almost luminescent. They possessed starflight, and had discovered humankind just a decade ago.

Since then there had been trade missions between Earth and Felekka, and guided tours on both worlds for politicians and scientists. And then an individual named Tahr, an artist, had requested a dome at Sapphire Oasis in which to work.

I sat patiently on the balcony, worked my way through the beers, and waited.

At eight, lights appeared on the long road which wound through the dunes towards the colony: a single limousine, escorted by a dozen motorcycle outriders. Their headlights mimicked a constellation, not unlike Orion, which oddly enough was from where the alien hailed.

Minutes later the gates of the Oasis eased open and the limousine swept inside. It drove sedately around the oasis and came to a gentle halt before the gaping crowd. The silence was absolute.

The chauffeur emerged quickly from the front of the car and opened a rear door. I heard the indrawn collective gasp of anticipation from the crowd and found myself leaning forward.

The chauffeur reached into the limousine, and I expected the figure of the alien to emerge.

In this I was disappointed, and at the same time intrigued.

The chauffeur pulled something from the rear of the vehicle, something hovering on an anti-grav sled, and drew it across the tesseraed apron of the oasis towards the dome set aside for the alien.

Something? At first I could not quite make out what it was. A case, a coffin? As the chauffeur passed beneath where I was sitting, I had a better view.

A cocoon, I thought. A dark brown, chitinous, torpedo-shaped pod... less manufactured, I thought, than *organic*. And then the chauffeur with his cargo passed into the scimitar support of the dome and disappeared from sight – much to the disappointment of the crowd and, I must admit, of myself.

In a mood of anti-climax I quit the balcony and returned to the studio. I stared at the crystal, then reached out... and experienced again my failure to bring the past to life.

Three years ago I had come to Sapphire Oasis with my wife, the opera singer Mariana De Vere. We had been married a year and already our relationship was faltering. How could two such great egos, the gossip columns had prophesied at the time of our marriage, cohabit without conflict?

The fact was that they could not.

I had thought I loved her, and at the time I probably had – but love possesses fluid properties, and changes with time. My love for Mariana had soon moved from being the product of intense physical passion, and the concomitant cerebral desire to possess her, to a mild affection, though still tinged with jealousy. She was immensely popular, and I was by nature insular and misanthropic, and I resented her giving of herself to others, not matter how innocent that giving might have been.

Perhaps that month at Sapphire Oasis had been an attempt to get to know each other again, to spend time together after our respective working tours. If so, it failed to work. Or perhaps it did work – we did get to know each other, and did not like what we found.

We argued. Christ, how we argued, and came to physical blows, and hurt each other in every possible way.

That night, that last night, she had accused me of producing work that was shallow and meretricious, steeped in a sickly sentimentalism that might have hoodwinked the more gullible critics, and the majority of the populace, but which failed to convince true aesthetes of its worth.

And perhaps what hurt so much was not that these criticisms came from the woman I had once loved, but I knew, in my heart, that what she said was true.

And I had countered in the only way possible, and accused her, perhaps baselessly, of having affair with the primitivist artist Ralph Standish. I had quipped that only an old man like Standish, over-blown and over-praised, could have found her attractive.

And she had fled the dome, sobbing, while I had remained and tried to lose myself in the production of another shallow, facile crystal.

In the morning I had been awoken by the manager of the dome, accompanied by the Oasis physician. They sat me down, and offered me a drink from my own bar, and told me that my wife's body had been found floating in the oasis at dawn.

The inquest returned a verdict of accidental death, but only I knew of the fragility of Mariana's mental state at the time; only I knew that just three days earlier she had threatened to take her own life if my insane and wholly unwarranted jealousy continued.

Now I reached for the crystal, the piece in which I had tried to imbue with the emotions of that night; my fear and jealousy and rage, overlaid with my abiding guilt... and as I ran my hands across the piece, I experienced only counterfeit emotions, pale shadows of what a real artist would have been able to create.

I nearly destroyed the piece then, but consequent events made me grateful that I did not.

I was awoken early by the persistent chime of the vidscreen. I sat up and swore. I was in the lounge, and fully clothed, and my head pounded in counterpoint to the summons of the 'screen.

I stabbed the *activate* stud aggressively. "What is it?"

"Christ, Ed, you look a sight for sore eyes."

I stared at the image on the screen. "Don't look too hot yourself," I said, and realised that my mouth was as dry as the Saharan sands.

It was Valigursky, my agent – the last person I wanted to see right then.

"Ed, ah... how's things?"

The enquiry was not at all altruistic: for 'how's things?' read: 'what are you working on?'

"Want the truth? I feel like shit, Sapphire is full of poseurs, and I'll never produce another crystal ever again. Does that answer your question?"

He looked worried, then vague. He was a bright kid in his early thirties, but the rich life – paid for by the twenty per cent he fleeced from me and other artists – had wrung him dry. First heroin, then spin, then MemErase. The sad bastard had had bits of his memory wiped when reality became too much and he had to off-load all the angst.

Mature individuals would have learned to live with the pain. Valigursky, being the shallow fool he was, had gone to Rio and employed the best neuro-sculptor to excise the offending thoughts and feelings.

Now he said, "You've claimed that before, Ed. You've often said you'd stop producing one day."

I grunted. "Sure. I'm saying it all the time." And I did, but how can an artist give up his work, even if that work *was* second rate?

I stared at Valigursky. "So... Can you remember what you called me for, or shall I cut the connection."

"No! I mean, I remember. Look, Henandez at the Prado was wondering if you had anything."

"Henandez? What happened to the private buyer?"

Almost four years ago, my work had suddenly become popular. Very popular.

Everything I did sold through a London gallery for increasingly excessive – I admit it – amounts. Not that I'd complained. But it had piqued my curiosity.

Enquiries discovered that a private buyer had taken a sudden liking to my work, and was buying it up – everything, even the early pieces.

Now I guessed that the private buyer had become disillusioned with my more recent, pathetic efforts, hence the Prado's enquiries.

Valigursky shrugged. "I don't know, Ed. Anyway, I say we go with Henandez –"

I cut in. "Anything you say, Val. You're the boss." I just wanted to get rid of him. "I'll crate up some of my latest pieces and ship them over, okay?"

Valigursky gave me a grin. "Good man, Ed!"

I reached out and killed the connection.

Seconds later the 'screen chimed again.

"Val, for Christ's sake –"

It wasn't Valigursky. The screen remained blank, but a voice said, "Edward Veron?"

"Yes?"

Something about the voice... I'd never heard anything like it before. Words formed by cobweb vocal chords and collapsed lungs.

Unearthly...

Or was that the wisdom of hindsight?

"Mr Veron? Perhaps we could meet?"

"Who is this?" I asked.

"I am Tahr, of Felekka, of the star you call Mintaka."

My breath caught. At last I said, "You want to see me?"

"If you would permit the intrusion."

"Sure... I mean, yes, of course. When?"

"I will come to your dome in three minutes, if that would be convenient."

I found myself saying, "By all means," and the connection went dead.

How do you prepare yourself to meet an alien?

Those days, I had trouble with members of my own species. I'd grown reclusive, even more misanthropic since Mariana's death. I found social interaction hard work and shunned people. How the hell was I to cope with an alien visitor?

Three minutes later, to the second, the door of the studio slid open and Tahr stepped inside.

The vid-shots and pix had not prepared me. The alien was tiny, perhaps the size of a ten year-old child, and slight. And though it was green, it was not as pale as I'd expected, but the almost luminescent green of a tree-frog.

It wore a white gown, toga-like, and moved slowly, almost warily.

But its face was the most disturbing aspect of its alienness.

It was reptilian, with faceted eyes like sieves on either side of its head, and mere hyphens for nostrils, and a long lipless mouth.

It paused and looked at me. Its great eyes nictitated, from the bottom up. "Edward Veron?" The voice was a whisper.

I nodded. "Please... take a seat." I indicated a chair beside my workbench.

"We... do not sit, my kind, but thank you."

"A drink, perhaps?"

"Water will be welcome."

As I drew two cups of chilled water from the cooler, I considered the reaction of the Oasis poseurs when they heard about my visitation.

"This is an honour," I said.

Tahr took the water in a green claw, and as I passed him the cup I ensured that our hands did not touch.

I leaned against the workbench.

"The honour is mine, Edward Veron. I am a great admirer of your work."

Was I still drunk? Was this some alcohol induced dream?

"You are?"

"Perhaps," it said, staggering me, "of all the artists of Earth which we have studied, we feel that your voice, what you have to say, most comprehensively represents what it is to be human. At least, what we *understand* it is like to be human."

I felt dizzy. I sat down. I took a long cold drink of water and felt better.

What the alien had told me opened up a lot of questions, of course; questions of perception, and comprehension, and cultural accessibility... But at that moment all I could think of was that I was big on Mintaka V.

I understood, then. "You... the Felekkans... *you're* the private buyers?"

"That is correct," Tahr said, "and that is why we are concerned."

I stared at it. "You are?"

"On Felekka," it said, "the most noble virtue is artistic integrity."

A dead-weight seemed to snag my heart and pull it down into my gut.

"Your latest work, Edward Veron, disappoints."

And the criticism, delivered by this strange alien, hurt me like no other: it was the verdict of his entire race, I felt, and I knew that it was true.

Perhaps only Mariana's words had cut so deep, before now.

"I... I've been unwell. I haven't been able to concentrate." It sounded like a plea for lenience, even to my own ears.

I had been back-peddling, producing on autopilot, cynically giving the audience what it wanted because I had been too lazy to give it what *I* wanted.

With remorseless logic, the alien continued, "Your latest phase dates from the death of your wife."

Tahr stared at me with its massive sieve-like eyes.

I stared back, dry-throated, unable to move a muscle.

I nodded. I almost used her death as an excuse, but the creature was wiser than that.

It said, "Perhaps you need to face your past with more honesty, Edward Veron, more *integrity*." And it stressed the final word.

Tahr moved, and before I could stop its progress with a shouted denial, it had crossed to my latest crystal and reached out.

It caressed the piece for about five minutes, standing absolutely still, apart from the rapid movement of its claws.

I could only look on, helpless, and filled with shame.

At last it moved away and looked at me. "This is weak, Edward Veron."

And I whispered, "I know."

"It is weak because it is not honest."

"I know."

"It is not honest," said my alien critic, "because you have not looked into your heart, or into your mind."

I stared at the alien, unable to say a word.

At last, Tahr said, "What is art, Edward Veron?"

The question surprised me. I thought, for a second, that I had been let off. "Where to begin?"

But the question had been rhetorical. The alien went on, "Art is the creation of that which allows others to perceive what it is to be human."

The silence, in the aftermath of this simple dictum, rang like a detonation.

And into the pool of that silence the alien dropped, "I can help you, Edward Veron. I can help you relive that night, and in reliving it so come to some understanding. Perhaps, with understanding, will come the ability to purge with art those feelings about yourself, and about your wife, which you have kept locked up for so long."

I shook my head. "How can you possibly do that?"

It gestured, reached out a hand, turned it. "I am an artist," it said, "and on Felekka, we artists have the ability to heal minds, and allow honesty to flow again. I can do that for you, if you wish."

I stared through the dome, away from the oasis, into the cruel and limitless expanse of the Sahara. It was desolate.

I said, "I don't know..."

"You wish to create again, to do your best, with integrity?"

"Of course."

"Then allow me to heal you, Edward Veron."

I hurried to the steps that gave access to the upper level of the dome. Halfway up, I turned. "I'll... I'll think about it."

The alien stepped from the studio and crossed the terrace to its own dome, much to the amazement of the on-looking artists.

I occluded the dome and sat in the twilight, held my head in my hands and considered what the alien had said.

And I thought back three years, to the night of Mariana's death, and the blank hours of darkness after the row, and my despair in the morning at being informed of my wife's suicide.

And was it any wonder that I had been unable to create since then? Was it any wonder that what I had put out had been dishonest, mediocre?

Perhaps Tahr was right, and I needed to face with honesty the events of that night.

And that afternoon, after many hours of anguish, I reached for the vidscreen and got through to the alien's dome.

"Please," I wept, "please help me."

That evening, at sunset, almost twenty four hours after arriving at Sapphire Oasis, Tahr the Felekkan entered my dome.

His earlier appearance had caused much discussion, and there was a crowd outside now to watch his unhurried transit.

He entered and I opaqued my dome from prying eyes.

"You have made the correct decision, Edward Veron."

"What now? How will you-?"

Tahr gestured to a foamform at the far side of the dome, where I had been in the habit of taking an afternoon rest. "Please, lie down."

Warily, I did so, watching the alien all the while. "What exactly," I said, "do you do?"

It was standing over me. I had never before felt so vulnerable, and a part of my mind panicked; but I was powerless to resist. It was as if I were paralysed by the gaze of its compound eyes.

It moved to the end of the foamform and stared down at me.

"Now I will take you back," it said.

And what it did then... I am shocked now to recall what happened, but I was even more shocked, and revolted, at the time.

Tahr bowed its head and opened its mouth, and something emerged from between its sunken lips, something I was convinced at the time was alive: a snake is the only Terran equivalent I can summon.

At any rate, before I could scream, or move away, the tentacle had thrust itself into my mouth, choking me, forcing itself down my throat, into my lungs, and seemed to expand, and with it came a sudden anaesthetic sensation, and I was floating, and no longer in pain, and then the scene of the alien's staring eyes dissolved, and I was no longer in my studio.

Memory flooded me... Except it was more than mere memory, more than simply reliving a scene recollected.

I was there, experiencing that night: it was as if I were a silent, involuntary passenger in the sensorium of my old self, mute and powerless to change what had happened... what was about to happen.

I was in the lounge, facing Mariana.

The sight of her took my breath away. She was there, alive, and beautiful, and the recollection of my love for her, and my hatred also, flooded me like physical pain.

"Come on, tell me!" I raged at her.

Her Latin eyes lasered into me. "You can be so childish, Eddy! So immature. You are a child, you know? You need a mother, not a wife!"

"Tell me!"

She cried, "Very well, I will: Your art is as shallow and immature as you, Eddy! Your very life is immature!"

"You always were a great critic," I said.

She shook her head. "Once, Eddy, you created great works. But lately you've become complacent, lazy."

I had heard enough. "Are you having an affair?" I asked.

The accusation so surprised her that she laughed. "What?"

"I said, Mariana, are you having an affair?"

She shook her head with something like incredulous wonderment. "Eddy... don't you see what you're doing? You can't even face up to the deficiency of your art! You think I criticise you because I've found someone else. What a fool you are!"

"Well, are you? Is it Standish, that old charlatan? Is he the only man you can attract these days?"

And staring at me with hating eyes, she backed from the dome, shaking her head, and ran away.

That was the last I recalled... the last I had allowed myself to recall.

But with Tahr's intervention, the truth was inescapable.

I followed her. It was three in the morning. The night was silent, and chill after the heat of the day. There was no one around. Even the lights of the domes which surrounded the oasis were dead.

I chased Mariana around the dome, consumed by rage, made even stronger when I guessed she was heading in the direction of Ralph Standish's dome.

And I caught up with her, and slapped her to the ground, and in a bid to escape from me she floundered into the oasis, and... God help me... but I reached out and with a strength made superhuman with insane rage and jealousy I held her head beneath the water as she struggling and fought, and then could struggle no more.

And then I returned to my dome, and awaited the inevitable outcome... except the outcome was not inevitable. The verdict concluded accidental death.

And my memory of what I had done?

The day after Mariana's drowning, I left Sahara Oasis and at Timbuktu caught a direct sub-orbital to Rio de Janeiro, and employed a neuro-sculptor to MemErase the previous twenty-four hours from my consciousness – and to erase the process of being MemErased, too.

So I had lost all memory of my sin, and much else beside.

When I came to my senses, the alien was standing on the far side of the dome, standing very still, watching me.

I felt no pain at his intrusion – no physical pain, that is.

I sat up. The alien turned. I gestured to stop it leaving.

As it moved to the sliding door, it turned to me and said, "On Felekka, Edward Veron, my art brings truth to the world, because truth is the only art."

And Tahr was gone.

That night, as the sun set and brought about another quick Saharan twilight, I sat on the verandah and watched the limousine pull up before the alien's dome. A crowd had gathered to watch, and heads were raised to where I sat. They wanted an explanation, but they would not get one, quite yet.

In time, the chauffeur emerged from the alien's dome, bearing the cocoon in which it lay, and drove sedately from the Oasis.

The extraterrestrial had done what it had come to Sapphire Oasis to do.

And I sat a while and watched the stars come out, and I looked back three years, and grieved.

Then I descended the steps to the studio and donned the glove and the wires. Fearful, I reached out to the incomplete crystal, and for the first time in years I resolved to imbue a creation with honesty, with *integrity* – and to face whatever consequences this might entail.

# Myths of the Martian Future

*There's a long if infrequent tradition in SF of tales in which crabs or crustaceans take centre stage. I can think of excellent stories by Robert Silverberg, Stephen Baxter, and Barington J. Bayley featuring shelled protagonists – and many more where aliens resemble crabs. There must be enough of them for some enterprising editor to gather in an anthology, perhaps with the title The Claws that Catch, or some such snappy title... Sorry. Anyway, here are my crab heroes, who happen to be Martians, about to set off on a brave quest across the torrid wastes of the red planet.*

At the end of the term, as was the custom among the Cave Dwellers, the two eldest males of the most recent hatching left the living chambers and made the long climb towards the surface of the planet.

Tem scuttled ahead through unfamiliar chambers, eager to begin the great adventure. Olinka, a little older and wiser, conserved his energy: great hardship lay ahead if they were to succeed in the Outside World.

As he climbed, Olinka considered the stories of their people, the Myths of the Outside, which many of his contemporaries took to be factual accounts of the exploits of Initiates long gone. He had thought long and hard about this, and was not so sure. He was not even convinced as to the reason for the Rite of Initiation: but he kept his doubts to himself. Tem was naive and headstrong, and Olinka did not want to quash his touching enthusiasm.

One tenth of a term after setting out, they came to the outer exit, and even Olinka felt a bubbling sense of expectancy somewhere within his shell.

He watched Tem scurry up the incline and pause in the circular opening. After the lambent illumination of the living chambers, the light from Outside was blinding. Olinka retracted his four eye-stalks and squinted at his friend. The sunlight struck Tem's etiolated shell and glanced off his six legs and madly waving pincers.

"The Outside World!" Tem signed. "It really is the Outside

World! I never thought I'd ever see..."

Olinka hurried up the incline and joined his friend on the ledge.

The first thing he saw was the sun. It was huge and majestic and filled half the sky, a ruddy dome on the circumference of which exploded slow-motion jets and geysers of flame. Beneath the ancient star, the land stretched away for as far as the eye could see, close at hand a rumple of foothills flattening out to a vast, red desert.

Olinka opened his right pincer in wonder as he made out movement in the sky.

He signalled to Tem: "Look! Is that a...? Can it be?"

"A Flyer, Olinka. Truly it is! A Flyer!"

Their eye-stalks tracked the great silver bird as it flapped with lazy economy across the baleful eye of the sun.

"And there – and there!" Olinka signed.

Tem was signalling: "Are they Burrowers, Olinka? There, those snub-nosed creatures in the valley! And those circular beasts making their way towards the desert! They must be Rollers!"

The Outside World was positively teeming with all manner of life! Olinka discerned perhaps a dozen strange life-forms down below – creatures he had heard described in the telling of the Myths: the Flyers, Rollers, and Burrowers. Among them were things that he could not name, shaggy, lumbering beasts that kept to the shadows, and slick, slithering legless things that basked on rocks in the glare of the sun. Only one creature had he ever actually *seen* before, deep within the living chambers, and the sight of it now filled him with a reassuring sense of familiarity. High in the air, patrolling the foothills in search of life-forms which might wish to communicate, was the many tentacled form of a Speaker.

He turned his eye-stalks towards the heavens and searched for other planets, but found none. Once, many thousands of terms ago, Initiates had reported witnessing the burning up of the solar system's third planet in the swelling wave-front of the expanding sun. And what of the people of that planet, Olinka had often wondered? Myth had it that, once, a proud race of bipeds had lived upon the third world. Another myth was that they had at one time visited this planet in strange, silver flying machines. Olinka wondered where truth finished and myth began.

They paused on the threshold of the Outside World. Tem

signalled: "You first, Olinka. You are my senior."

"I could not stand in the way of youthful enthusiasm," Olinka signed with a hint of condescension. "You first."

Nimble with importance, eye-stalks quivering with excitement, Tem stepped from the shadow of the exit.

He semaphored the words of the Initiates upon Emerging: "We stand upon the cusp of adventure. We will be judged by our exploits. We ask nothing more than to return with tales to add to those of our illustrious forbears!"

Olinka kept his limbs, pincers, and eye-stalks scrupulously immobile. The words of Emerging were nothing more than sentimental rubbish, but he was reluctant to tell Tem of his reasons for thinking so.

He followed his friend carefully down the hillside towards the desert, picking his way over and around the tumbled scree. The heat of the sun smote his shell like something physical, and Olinka wondered how he might survive ten terms of such inimical onslaught. Ten terms! If he were lucky, he might live for a hundred terms. And he was expected to survive out here for a tenth of a lifetime!

Five tenths of a term after leaving the mountain, Olinka and Tem arrived at the desert. Tem, eager as ever, scurried up the sliding face of a wind-sculptured dune. At the top he stood high and proud on his six bandy legs and waved his eye-stalks impatiently for Olinka to join him.

Olinka navigated the curve of the dune and arrived beside his friend.

They had completed the first stage of their Initiation. Now they had an important choice to make, one which countless Initiates had made before them. The consensus of opinion was that to venture out into the merciless heat of the desert was risky indeed: few who made the journey returned to tell the tale. However, those few that did emerge triumphant from the ordeal by fire came back with stirring stories of valour and sacrifice, stories which immeasurably enriched the history of the Cave Dwellers. The Initiates who took the safer option, the circumnavigation of the mountain via the foothills, brought back less colourful tales, and these Initiates, and their stories, were often forgotten in the long march of time.

Now Tem signalled: "Olinka?"

"Yes, Tem?"

"Do you know what I am thinking?"

"Hmmm... I can guess."

"And you?"

"I think you know what I suggest, Tem."

In high dudgeon, Tem signed: "What, Olinka? That we go around the mountain like timid hatchlings? Encounter what every thin-blooded Initiate has encountered before, and which every one of our people has forgotten?"

"Yes, rather that than face the uncertainties of the desert. The dangers –"

"But we can overcome the dangers, Olinka. We are young and strong!"

"Youth will not save us from the Eaters," Olinka pointed out. "Nor will our strength. The Eaters will take great delight in plucking our limbs one by one from our shells and sucking out our brains!"

Tem brought all four of his eye-stalks to bear on Olinka. "What do you think is the reason for Initiation, then?" he signalled with acerbity. "Nothing is gained without risk. What is glory without the possibility of sacrifice!"

Angered, Olinka brought both his pincers up to eye-level, for emphasis, and began: "Do you really want to know what I think Initiation is for, Tem?" He almost stopped himself, there. But his friend's short-sightedness, his lack of insight, had angered him for many terms now. Tem had always gone with the flow, accepting whatever the Elders said, without thought or question. Now it was time to put him right.

Olinka continued: "Initiation is not what you think it is. It is not a means to provide our people with a history, with knowledge of the Outside World. Think about it. Consider the conditions in the living chambers. The fact is that our chambers and galleries are overcrowded. There is hardly enough food or water for everyone. It is a fact that males outnumber females almost six to one. Is it any wonder that only males are sent out on these great Initiations?"

Tem backed away, retracting his eye-stalks in horror. "What are you saying?" he signed with his left rear leg, to denote shock and disbelief.

Olinka allowed a profound immobility to reign. Then he signalled:

"I am saying that the Initiations are no more than a means by which our society regulates its numbers, a means of culling unwanted males, to ensure the survival of those who remain in the living chambers."

Tem shuffled sideways, putting distance between himself and the heretic notions of his fellow Initiate. "I cannot accept that! I will not accept..." His pincer was still. Then he waved: "But what about the Initiates who do return with magnificent tales of brave deeds?"

Olinka gestured, placating. "I do not deny that these stories add to the richness of our culture – but how many males return, Tem? Six from every twenty? Which means that fourteen perish. Can you deny that our society is better off for the sacrifice of these Initiates?" He stopped, suddenly, and stared ahead.

At first he thought that it was a trick of his eye-stalks. He made out a slight irregularity on the northernmost fringe of the desert, a silver filament that seemed stationary. He looked away for a few seconds, and then glanced back. Certainly the filament had moved a fraction, was heading into the heart of the desert.

"What is it?" Tem asked.

"Look..."

The column was many thousands of body-lengths distant, and consisted of perhaps a hundred silver-grey individuals. They walked on four legs beneath cupola-shaped head-bodies, and from their craniums sprouted two eye-stalks.

"I don't believe I'm seeing this!" Tem signed.

"Do you think...?" Olinka began. "Can they be?"

He turned his gaze skyward, looking for the tentacled shape of a Speaker. The bloated belly of the sun filled sky, and against its light Olinka made out the relatively tiny shape of a floating Speaker. He signalled frantically, requesting that it descend and communicate with them.

Just when he thought that the creature had not seen his summons, or was ignoring him, the Speaker turned and swooped towards the dune.

It hung above their heads, its tentacles working in a passable imitation of their language.

"Two shell-heads, out in the open! How can I help you, Initiates?"

Olinka signalled: "The beings crossing the desert, there. Are they what I think they are, Speaker?"

The Speaker rotated to consider the column, but Olinka could not tell the difference between its tentacles and eye-stalks. At last it signed: "If you think that they are Thinkers, Initiate, then they are what you think they are."

Olinka felt the blood surge around his head-shell. His six legs were suddenly weak.

Tem signalled frantically: "Thinkers! Are they *really* Thinkers?"

The Speaker signed: "They are Thinkers from the north, making their annual pilgrimage to the Southern Plain. There they will commune with the oracles, and contemplate the vast history of the planet for one long year before returning to their breeding grounds."

"Thinkers..." Olinka gestured in awe.

The history of the Cave Dwellers was so vast that few stories reached them from the time when they had lived on the surface of the world. One story, however, had survived. It was a tale so fabulous that it had to be a myth.

It was said that long ago, a million generations in the past, the Thinkers and the race which eventually became the Cave Dwellers were one and the same. A clan of Thinkers, so the story went, returning from their annual pilgrimage, had been caught in a sunstorm, and in order to wait out the worst of the actinic sleet had sought refuge in the caves of the central mountains. Quite why they had remained in the mountain, and moved further underground with every passing generation, was never adequately explained. According to the story, the Thinkers changed, became shorter, and grew more legs and eye-stalks and pincers, and became in time the Cave Dwellers. It was a strange and unlikely story, Olinka thought, but one which contained much poignancy.

To imagine that the Cave Dwellers might be descended from the mighty Thinkers, the ancient philosopher race which existed in some abstract realm of pure thought and reason!

Now Tem signalled impetuously. "Speaker! We require your assistance."

Olinka spun and stared at his friend with all four eye-stalks. "We do?"

Tem ignored him. "Will you accompany us into the desert, Speaker, and translate whatever might pass between ourselves and the venerable Thinkers?"

The floating being signed: "They call me a Speaker because I speak, little one. I will follow you into the great desert."

"Wait!" Olinka gestured with two pincers in his most determined manner. "Who said anything about –?"

Tem turned and stared. "We must follow them! Don't you see that we cannot let this opportunity pass? Think of it, Olinka: we will determine once and for all the truth of our ancestry. We will be famous in every living chamber! Our names will never be forgotten and our story will enrich the history of our people!"

Olinka turned to the patiently floating Speaker. "Please recount for the benefit of my headstrong friend the dangers awaiting us in the great desert."

The Speaker descended and hovered before Tem. "The dangers are indeed great for two puny little shell-heads such as yourselves."

"We can defend ourselves with these," Tem gestured, brandishing his pincers in demonstration.

The Speaker signed much humour. "Against a ravenous Eater, your claws will be useless! Also, the Thinkers move at prodigious speed, and stop for no one. You will have difficulty catching them."

"That is a risk we will have to face," Tem signed, "along with the danger. Glory beckons! How can we turn our backs like two hatchlings on such an opportunity?"

Something in Olinka stirred. He thought of their reception, back in the living chambers, if indeed they did succeed in communicating with the Thinkers.

"Two terms," he gestured. "We will attempt to catch up with the column, but after two terms, if we have not overhauled them, then we turn back."

Tem hesitated, then waved a pincer in agreement. "Two terms, then," he signed, and scurried off down the face of the dune.

Gesturing to himself, the Speaker hovering overhead, Olinka gave chase.

For the duration of the next term, Olinka hurried alongside Tem in a foam of excitement and apprehension. Ahead, the shimmering column of Thinkers remained hopelessly distant. He willed himself to greater speed, or the column to slow, so they might achieve their aim and quiz the venerable beings, and then return in safety to the foothills. With every passing second he expected something vast and vicious to erupt from the sand beside him and attack with savage tooth and claw. He had heard many fearsome stories about the Eaters. As a hatchling he had listened with terror as the Wise Elders described in grotesque detail the dining habits of the desert dwellers.

The Thinkers seemed to draw no nearer, and almost two terms had elapsed when Tem paused in his headlong flight and strained his eye-stalks ahead. "They move with the speed of Flyers!" he gestured, exasperated.

"It is time we turned and headed back," Olinka signed, in sympathy, and not a little regret.

Tem ignored him. He gestured to the Speaker. "Will you fly ahead, Speaker? Inform the column that we wish an audience."

The Speaker dipped before the Initiates. He gestured great mirth. "The Thinkers pause in their pilgrimage for no one, great or small, little ones."

Tem stamped in annoyance. "Tell them that we are descended from their kind, and wish to speak with them!"

Again the Speaker signed humour. "The Thinkers might take offence that two shell-heads claim such a heritage," it gestured. "Be satisfied that your eye-stalks have beheld such a procession, and that so far you have lived to tell the tale!"

"Come, Tem," Olinka gestured. "We will continue our Initiation in the foothills."

He turned, touching his friend's carapace with a consolatory claw, and they began the long trek back to the mountain. He looked into his heart, and admitted to himself that he too felt the burden of sadness at the fruitless outcome of the mission.

He was about to remind Tem that they had much time in which to accomplish notable deeds when, ahead, in the first gentle fold of the foothills, he saw a quick flash of light.

He turned his eye-stalks in that direction, and beheld a large floating craft shaped like a water droplet, coruscating silver in the sunlight.

It was leaving the foothills and crossing the desert towards them.

Tem gave a gesture of fright and rapidly buried himself in the sand. Olinka twisted himself beneath the surface of the desert, then extended a periscopic eye-stalk to track the craft's slow progress.

A rectangular section at the front of the droplet-shaped vehicle was made of some transparent material. Olinka made out two short, upright figures within the craft. One of the strange beings seemed to be directing the craft with a limb connected to a column, which it moved in the direction it wished the craft to follow.

Olinka wondered at the marvel of happening upon the column of Thinkers, and then this strange sight, so soon after leaving the mountain.

The craft approached the buried Cave Dwellers and passed quickly overhead. Olinka bent his eye-stalk to follow. Much to his excitement, the vehicle soon slowed and lowered itself to the ground. It sat immobile on the sand beneath the fierce sun, perhaps a hundred body-lengths away.

Then, startling him, a section of the droplet-shaped craft sprang open like the wing of an insect. Olinka watched with excitement. Beside him, he discerned Tem's timorous eye-stalk, taking in the scene.

As he watched, two silver beings stepped from the craft and stood looking about them, and Olinka could not contain his excitement.

He shrugged all his eye-stalks, and a pincer, free of the sand and communicated with Tem.

"Do you think it could be?" he asked. "Do you really think...?"

Tem was slow in responding, as if dazed by the marvel unfolding before them.

"It can only be," he signalled. "It can only be the Silver Travellers!"

Olinka turned his eye-stalks forward and watched as the Silver Travellers strode around their craft, sometimes pausing to examine the desert floor, sometimes gazing up at the swollen sun.

Olinka felt his life-blood surge as he recalled the story of the Silver Travellers. It was an old tale, the details lost in the long history of their people. Many hundreds of thousands of terms ago, so the story went, two eager Initiates had ventured forth from the mountain and decided to cross the desert to the Southern Plain. It was a foolhardy choice to make, and one bound to end in disaster, as no Cave Dweller had ever set eye-stalks on the far distant flatland or the oracles said to reside there.

These two Initiates, however, were far from daunted. The story, no doubt much embroidered over time, went into great detail about the hardships they endured as they crossed the desert, the many perils they faced from predators and foe.

After seven terms beneath the merciless intensity of the sun, the two heroes weakened. They realised the absurdity of their attempt, and realised also the impossibility of turning back. They resigned themselves to death, and were about to bury themselves in the sand and await the end when, as if their plight was not dire enough, they were swooped upon by a pack of Eaters.

One of the Initiates was riven limb from pincer before the terrified eye-stalks of his friend. The victim's shell was prised open by the Eaters' eager claws, his brain laid bare for the delectation of the ravenous beasts.

The surviving Initiate felt the claws of an Eater grab him. He was ready for death – but instead came salvation.

He was aware of commotion about him. He was dropped suddenly, and went rolling in ever decreasing circles around the desert floor, realising as he did so that the Eaters were fleeing in fright. When he came to rest, he saw the reason for their sudden departure.

Two tall, upright silver figures stood over him. One knelt and reached out a limb, which terminated in five small digits.

Frightened, the Cave Dweller summoned a Speaker, and communicated with the silver beings. The beings were first amazed by the fact of the Cave Dweller's sentience, and then saddened by his companion's death.

The remaining Initiate asked if the silver beings might transport him back to the foothills in their craft, and they agreed. They ferried him safely to the entrance in the foothills, and thus ensured not only his survival, but one of the most famous rites of Initiation ever undertaken by a cave Dweller.

There was much speculation as to the provenance of the Silver Travellers. Some claimed that the beings were helpful ghosts, others that they were survivors who had fled the destruction of the system's third planet.

Olinka had always considered the story more myth than fact, a far-fetched farrago of improbabilities concocted in the sun-crazed mind of an over-adventurous Initiate.

But here, before him, were two strange silver beings very much like those of ancient myth.

"Should we approach them?" Olinka signalled to Tem, "attempt communication?" He scanned the sky for the Speaker.

"We might introduce ourselves!" Tem signed, excited.

The Silver Travellers were walking away from the craft, scanning the ground with strange instruments. From time to time they turned to each other, as if in communication – though the movement of their limbs was minimal. Olinka wondered how such obviously sentient creatures might effect communication with just four rudimentary limbs which seemed to lack anything but the most simple flexibility.

Olinka had sighted the Speaker high in the sky, and was about to ask its assistance, when disaster struck.

He felt the sand tremble around him, and thought at first that it was a quake similar to those which occasionally shook the mountain. Then the sand of the desert, in an approximate ring encompassing the two Silver Travellers, erupted and a dozen creatures, the like of which Olinka had never seen before, emerged and made for the two unwitting beings.

Olinka stared in horror, knowing full well that he was helpless to intervene. The creatures were attenuated, insect-like monsters twice as tall as the Silver Travellers, all jet-black chitin and massive mandibles. Olinka expected them to devour the silver beings straight away, but the insects had other plans.

Four of their swarm took hold of the frantically struggling beings, spread their iridescent wings and bore them off into the air, followed by the remaining insects. They passed overhead and made for the foothills, the Silver Travellers dangling.

Tem was flailing his limbs in an incomprehensible welter of sadness and grief.

"We have to help them!" Olinka signed.

"Impossible! What are we beside those vile monsters?"

Olinka, without quite knowing what he intended, leaped from his hiding place in the sand and hurried across the desert towards the droplet-shaped craft. Tem scuttled in his wake, signalling a dozen frantic questions.

He reached the open hatch of the vehicle, hesitated only briefly, and then jumped inside. Before he knew it, Tem was beside him. "Have you taken leave of your senses, Olinka? What are you doing?"

"I saw how the beings directed this craft," Olinka signed. He reached out with his pincer and touched the column before him. No sooner had his claw made contact than the hatch swung shut and the craft bobbed sickeningly into the air.

With mounting fear, Olinka watched through the viewscreen as the desert receded beneath him. Tem huddled on the floor, his limbs, pincers and eye-stalks waving in garbled distress.

Olinka fought the sensation of sickness that threatened to overwhelm him. He pushed at the column, as he had seen the Silver Traveller do, and the craft responded. It surged forward, almost pitching Olinka to the floor. He eased the column to the right, turning the craft in the direction of the foothills.

They were flying! They were the first Cave Dwellers ever to take control of a flying machine! Olinka marvelled at the miracle, hardly daring to believe what was happening. What stories they would have to tell their people. Their exploits would be remembered for ever! Their names would never be forgotten!

If, he reminded himself, they survived to tell the tale.

Ahead, through the viewscreen, he made out the distant flight of insect-monsters, their dependent prey flashing in the sunlight. The insects swarmed across the desert towards the foothills. As Olinka gave chase, the beasts suddenly lost altitude and settled in an amphitheatre enclosed by hills. As he watched, even more of the insect creatures emerged from holes in the ground.

Those carrying the Silver Travellers swooped in to land. Olinka knew that soon the opportunity to save the beings would be gone, once the insects took the captives to their underground lair.

He pushed the column forward and the craft dived.

"What are you doing?" Tem signalled in alarm.

Olinka was fuelled by the desire to save the Silver Travellers, to do for them what their kind had done for the Initiate, long ago – if that story was to be believed. Quite how he might effect such a rescue, he did not know. He was running on instinct, blind hope, and fear.

They fell towards the amphitheatre.

The insects had landed and were scurrying across the sun-browned grass towards the nearest hole in the ground.

The craft came into the amphitheatre on a low trajectory, skimming the grass and heading towards the first of the insect-monsters.

"Hold tight!" Olinka warned Tem.

Through the viewscreen he beheld the looming shapes of a dozen insects, and then came the inevitable collision. The craft skittled the creatures and flew on erratically. Olinka beheld halved insects littering the ground, and others, badly injured, attempting to crawl away. Ahead, he made out the insects bearing the Silver Travellers, and steered the craft full-tilt towards them. This time the impact, when it came, was jarring and final. There was a shell-shaking vibration, and then sudden immobility. He and Tem rattled around the interior of the craft, tumbling on top of each other in a tangle of legs and eye-stalks.

Dazed, Olinka stood unsteadily and stared about him. Chitinous shrapnel and viscous ichor covered the viewscreen. Through a clear segment, he made out a scene of carnage, with fragments of insect shell scattered over a wide area.

As he stared, he heard the hatch open above him, and knew that the end had come. He hoped only that it would be swift, that the surviving insects would devour him quickly rather than desire to exact revenge.

He turned an eye-stalk and looked up, and what he saw filled him with disbelief. A silver being was holding the hatch open and staring into the craft with two flat, round eyes. Its strange headpiece was enclosed within a bulbous, transparent shell, which was connected by two pipes to a bulky apparatus upon its back.

Olinka wished he could have made sense of the expression on the ugly headpiece as the Traveller took in the jumbled interior of its craft, and the two tiny Cave Dwellers who had effected their salvation.

The face disappeared, and a second later the craft was righted, Olinka and Tem falling to the floor.

"What's happening!" Tem signalled. "Are we dead yet!"

Olinka had no time to reply. Through the viewscreen he made out the amphitheatre. Panic seized him and his limbs signalled danger, as if the two Travellers might comprehend.

Across the amphitheatre, the surviving insects were gathering their forces to attack. As Olinka watched in dread, they launched themselves towards the craft. He turned his eye-stalks towards the hatch. He saw one Traveller kneeling beside the craft, perhaps attempting some form of repair. The second Traveller looked up, saw the approaching insects, and signalled to his friend.

They climbed quickly into the craft and slammed the hatch shut behind them, and not a moment too soon. The insects were swarming over the droplet-shaped vehicle, mandibles working to open its skin.

One of the Travellers reached out for the control column, eased it forward. Olinka was aware of a stalling vibration. The ship did not respond.

Outside, the craft was engulfed in a swarm of insects. Tem gestured in fear. Olinka felt the craft rock as the insects attempted to crack it open.

The first Traveller turned to the second. On its face, within the transparent shell, two thin strips of flesh surrounding a pink orifice made a minimal movement. Olinka found it amazing that such restricted gestures might convey any meaningful language.

The first being reached beyond the control column to a panel arrayed with tiny hieroglyphs. With its thin appendages, the Traveller tapped the console.

Instantly, the insects crowding the viewscreen disappeared, and light flashed outside the craft. Olinka felt suddenly nauseous. His limbs buckled and he slid towards Tem in the corner of the craft. He was aware of a constant vibration that threatened to shake his shell to fragments. He retracted his eye-stalks and took refuge in darkness.

Then, just as suddenly as it had started, the nausea ceased. The vibration was no more. Cautiously, Olinka extended an eye-stalk and peered around him.

All was immobile. The sun shone through the viewscreen. He looked out. All across the amphitheatre lay the remains of shattered insects, wing-cases and antennae, severed heads and legs. He looked away.

The Silver Travellers opened the hatch and climbed out. One reached back inside, picked up first Olinka, and then Tem, and lifted them out into the sunlight.

The Traveller placed Olinka and Tem side by side on the grass, then knelt to stare at the tiny Cave Dwellers.

Olinka scanned the heavens for a Speaker. Within seconds his signals brought a response. A tentacled Speaker swooped to join them.

"The two shell-heads survive!" the Speaker gestured in patronising disbelief. "You'll be heroes when your people hear of your exploits!"

"You followed us from the desert?" Olinka signed.

"Oh, it's more complicated than that, my friends!"

Tem signalled: "We wish to communicate with the Silver Travellers."

"And they," responded the Speaker, "wish to communicate with you!"

The first Traveller looked up at the floating Speaker. Again, the being moved the fleshy strips on its headpiece.

The Speaker rotated and addressed Olinka and Tem. "They wish to thank you," it signed. "Without your intervention, they would now be dead."

"Tell them," Olinka signalled, flashing pincers and limbs in joy, "that it was the least we could do. Many terms ago, so rumour has it, two of their kind also saved a Cave Dweller from certain death."

The Speaker turned to address the Travellers. There followed a period of immobility. The Speaker did not use its tentacles to communicate, and Olinka was confused.

However, the Speaker must have conveyed Olinka's words, for they had an immediate effect. The two Travellers turned to each other. Their headpieces shook from side to side and their fleshy strips moved animatedly.

The Speaker relayed what they had said. "They wish to tell you that it was *they* who saved your forbears in the desert."

"They?" Olinka responded. "But... how is that possible? It was many hundreds of terms ago! Surely no beings can live that long?"

Impatiently, Tem signalled to the Speaker. "Ask the Silver Travellers where they are from."

The Speaker conveyed the question, its tentacles immobile. The Travellers moved their heads, manipulated their inefficient signing strips.

At last the Speaker signalled: "They come, originally, from a place they call Earth – the third planet of this system."

"But their planet was destroyed, or so the story goes," Olinka signed. "Where do they dwell now?"

The Travellers were communicating again.

The Speaker reported: "Long ago they fled their planet when it was threatened by the expansion of the sun. Now, they travel through time," the Speaker went on. "They move through the long history of the solar system in their machine, alighting to study the many and various forms of life."

"Travel through *time*...?" Olinka gestured, awed at the concept.

"How else do you think that they might have saved your distant forbear?" the Speaker asked.

Olinka's thoughts were in turmoil. He wished to ask the Travellers a thousand questions. He considered the many events since leaving the mountain. He recalled the column of Thinkers, and remembered the myth.

"If the Travellers do indeed travel through time," he signed to the Speaker, "then perhaps they might be able to answer my question?"

"And that is?"

Olinka turned his eye-stalks and snapped his pincers. "Do they know if it is true," he began, "that once, many millions of terms ago, we Cave Dwellers were one and the same as the Thinkers?"

As he waited for the Speaker to relay the question to the time-travelling bipeds, he thought ahead to their triumphal return to the living chambers, and the stories they would have to recount.

Perhaps, even, they might be able to report with certainty that their people were indeed descended from the venerable Thinkers!

The Travellers moved their fleshy strips. Olinka was aware of a dizziness within his shell as he awaited the reply.

"Over many millennia," the Speaker signed at last, "the Thinkers have made an annual pilgrimage to the Southern Plain. The time travellers have monitored their journeys-"

"But are we descended from the Thinkers?" Tem was impatient to know.

"Sadly," the Speaker signed, "this is a groundless myth of your people. You are descended from lowly crustaceans which have always lived beneath the surface of the planet."

Olinka felt a crushing sense of disappointment. How might they return, now, with news that one of their long-held and most cherished stories was no more than a fanciful fairy tale?

He felt that all his exploits since leaving the mountain might have been for nothing.

Beside him, Tem's pincers drooped in eloquent dejection.

The Travellers were communicating again. The Speaker turned. "They say that you should not be disappointed," it gestured. "For not only have they knowledge of your distant past – but also they know the course of your future."

"They do?" Tem signed in disbelief.

"The only way they have of thanking you for saving their lives," the Speaker continued, "is to tell you to return to your living chambers and inform your people that, one day, your race will be great. You will leave your subterranean lair and live out in the open, under the sun. Then will begin the long period of your greatness. Over many terms, your kind will populate every corner of the planet, and become philosophers on par with and even exceeding the venerable Thinkers."

Olinka's legs buckled and he collapsed to the ground. With his pincers he gestured: "They know this? They know this for sure?"

The Speaker replied: "They told me that the planet will never know of a race as intelligent and civilised as the people once known as the Cave Dwellers."

For once, Olinka was speechless. He could not bring himself to move his limbs in any semblance of order.

"And now," the Speaker reported, "the Travellers must leave this period. They wish you well, and thank you once again."

The first biped reached out a long limb, extending its digits towards Olinka. Not knowing quite how to respond, but sensing that some gesture was required, he lifted his right pincer and gently touched the tip of the Traveller's digit, and repeated the gesture with the second creature.

The fleshy strips upon the Travellers' headpieces curled into a shape that might have been significant.

The Travellers stood, and lifted their limbs at Olinka and Tem, before climbing back into the time machine.

Olinka directed his eye-stalks forward, overcome with sadness as the hatch closed. He expected to watch it fly away, but instead it vanished in a flash of light, disappeared once again on its mysterious errand through time.

Tem was beside himself with delight. He danced up the side of the amphitheatre, heading towards the entrance to the living chambers. His limbs flashed in glee, and Olinka made out brief phrases. "One day we will be great! Together, Olinka and I will lead our people from the living chambers! One day we will be *great*!"

Olinka, with the Speaker in attendance, followed Tem up the hillside.

Tem paused in his celebratory jig. "You will accompany us into the chambers, Speaker? You will corroborate the many wonderful stories Olinka and I have to tell our people?"

"I am a Speaker. That is my duty."

Olinka halted his friend with a gesture. "But we cannot return to the living chambers so soon," he signed. "The Elders will never believe us! We have been away hardly three terms!"

He was aware of the Speaker above them, signing his mirth.

"What?" Olinka asked.

The Speaker gestured. "You cannot guess?"

"Guess what?" Tem signed.

"How do you think you evaded the insect-monsters?" it asked. "Where do you think the insects vanished to, all of a sudden?"

Tem shrugged a pincer. Olinka recalled the nausea he had experienced in the craft, the eerie flashing light.

"Tell us, Speaker," he signed.

"To escape the remaining insects," it signed, "the Travellers moved the craft through *time*. The insects either died of their wounds in the interim, or fled."

Olinka marvelled at the very idea. At last he found himself gesturing: "For how long did we travel through time?"

The Speaker responded: "A little over thirty terms."

*Thirty terms*! An Initiation was supposed to last only ten!

Olinka thought of his friends back in the chambers, the Wise Elders who had counselled them over the terms. They would have assumed the worst, by now. They would think that brave Initiates Olinka and Tem had left the mountain and met with a tragic end.

Their return would be a triumph indeed. Oh, the tales they would have to tell...

Already Tem was skipping nimbly up the mountainside, followed by the floating Speaker.

Olinka, bursting with pride and joy, set off in pursuit.

# The Scribe of Betelgeuse V

*This story began life as a one thousand word short-short – comprising the first section of the present story. It sat in my files a while until I realised, belatedly, that there was more story to tell. However, to do that I would have to employ two further viewpoint characters – not the done thing in a tale a little under four thousand words. But rules are made to be broken... It's another story about a visitor from the stars bringing about change, though this time not for the better. It's tongue-in-cheek humorous, and I enjoyed poking gentle fun at the publishing industry.*

*One: Hemmings*

The block began on Monday morning.

I sat down before the glowing screen of my trusty PC, found the file containing the final chapter of the novel I was working on – and stalled.

The words just would not come. I tried everything. Pacing my study. Reading passages from my favourite books. I even tapped out a few lines of gibberish, just to get me started. Nothing worked.

Now, I'm a full-time freelance writer. I write novels, short stories and the occasional screenplay. I've never subscribed to the idea of writer's block. It's a luxury, the neurotic affectation of scribblers who pen effete vignettes and rarefied literary memoirs.

The fact was, I couldn't afford to be blocked.

I decided to go out for a coffee.

I was on my second cup when a silence fell over the café, broken only by the murmur of the radio. The proprietor turned up the volume.

"... reports coming in from all over the world of vast vessels appearing above major cities..."

Someone stood up, knocking over his chair, and dashed outside with a cry. People in the street were gesturing skywards. I peered out, shocked to see the immense shape of a silver spaceship sliding over

Highgate and blotting out the sun.

Suddenly, my writer's block didn't seem very important.

I returned home, in the shadow of the looming spaceship, and switched on the TV.

All the channels carried pictures of the alien ships, along with reassurances from our political leaders that they had the situation 'under control'.

I fired off a few e-mails to the SF writers I knew – snarky barbs along the lines of: "Yah – what'll you write about now?"

Keith Brooke got back to me instantly. "Good point. Time for that chic-lit novel, I reckon. With aliens. But actually, I haven't been able to write a word for a couple of days. Damn it, I'm blocked!"

I replied, commiserating, and saying that if it were any consolation, then so was I.

The phone rang. It was Carstairs, my agent.

"I know, I've seen it," I said, forestalling his pronouncement of the obvious.

"Actually, I wasn't phoning about the Betelgeusians, Hemmings, dear boy –"

"The Betelgeusians?"

"Tune into BBC News. There's been word from the aliens. They're Betelgeusians – not that they call themselves that. Their name for themselves runs to around twenty syllables, or so I gather."

"So if you weren't ringing about the aliens...?"

"Oh – the novel, of course. It was due on my desk last week, in case you've forgotten."

"Ah..."

"You're not blocked, are you?"

"Blocked? Me? Of course not! Why do you ask?"

"It's just that it's seemingly fashionable these days. Half a dozen of my clients have reported being deserted by the muse. Oh, the travails of an agent! Very well, then. I'll expect the manuscript a week today. Toodle-pip."

I swore at the phone and switched to BBC News.

I was just in time to see footage of the ship landing in London. A ramp came down and a creature – a Betelgeusian, or whatever they called themselves – appeared in the entrance.

The alien was an octopus, a blue octopus splashed liberally with red spots. It was joined by others, tentacles waving.

Floating by the first alien's head was a silver box, into which the creature spoke.

Seconds later a translation filled the air of Hyde Park. "Citizens of Earth, we come in peace!"

Reassured, I returned to my PC and tried to crack on with that last chapter.

For the life of me, I couldn't produce a damned word.

I gave in and watched the TV broadcast.

By the end of the day, the Prime Minister had inveigled himself into a photo-opportunity with Glag, the leader of the aliens. Pictures of him shaking the ET's tentacles were all over the morning papers.

At nine, I dutifully sat before my purring PC and tried to kick life into that final chapter. I should have found it easy. The scene was set, the hero on the edge of peril, with a neat finale and twist-in-the-tail worked out – but the essential commodity, the words, refused to appear.

The phone rang. If it's Carstairs, I told myself, I'll hang up...

It was Ian Whates, friend, writer and editor. "Ian, how's things?"

"I'm blocked. Would you believe it? Can't write a word. Not a thing. And what's more, it isn't just me."

I felt as if I'd been kicked in the gut by a vicious mule. "It isn't?"

"I've been bombarded by e-mails from friends in the business. They're all in the same boat. Can't write a word. I was just online. The blogs are abuzz. Strange thing is, journos and the like are okay – it's just us fiction writers. What about you?"

I was silent for a second or two, recovering. "Me too."

"I'll be in touch if I hear anything else."

Before I'd even begun to order my thoughts in the wake of Ian's call, the phone rang again. This time it *was* Carstairs.

"I thought I told you...!" I began.

"Calm down, dear boy. Look, can you get into the office, quick sharpish? Something rather juicy has come up..."

'Something Juicy' in Carstairs-speak meant dosh. I said I'd be around within the hour.

I sat in Carstairs' office, staring through the window. I could just see the silver dome of the alien ship in the distance.

"I've been made a rather delicious offer," Carstairs was saying with the air of a man who can't quite believe his luck. He tapped a CD on his desk. "A novel."

"And?"

"I'm looking for someone to... ah... cut it down somewhat. It's far too long as it stands, could do with a little paring, shall we say? If you could shave around eighty thousand words, the job's yours for ten grand. Of course, for that kind of advance you can't expect royalties..."

It was money for jam, even sans royalties.

"But who wrote it? Won't they object to having eight kay excised?"

Carstairs pointed to a wall-mounted flatscreen. It showed a fat octopus at a party in Mayfair, clutching at least four glasses of champagne.

"The leader of the Betelgeusians who landed in London is a novelist. He wants to sell his latest here on Earth. I got in ahead of agencies all over the globe. I have a publisher interested... so if you could get it done by Friday."

I hesitated. "What about my novel?"

Carstairs smiled to himself. "Your novel? Forget it, dear boy."

The following morning, at nine on the dot, I powered up my PC, inserted the CD, and began work.

The opening line of the alien scribe's masterpiece ran thus:

*Jix pondered with laborious deliberation whether he might consider a leisurely swim through the glume swamps, where if he were of sufficient good fortune he might make the acquaintance of Zeep.*

Which I reworked as: *Jix pondered a swim through the glume swamps, where he might make the acquaintance of Zeep.*

The night before I'd attempted to work on the last chapter of my novel, but the words had been elusive.

Now, the arrival of the aliens and the concurrent world-wide block on novelist's creativity had to be linked, surely?

If so, then how were they doing it? And, more worryingly, *why*...

*Two: Carstairs*

I met Fletcher, the commissioning editor at Greenwood and Worley, a couple of days after the Betelgeusians arrived on Earth.

"But how did you manage to secure the…" He gestured to the manuscript on his desk.

"I have friends in high places," I said. "Very high places. I was at a party thrown by the PM to welcome the aliens. I got talking to Glag, their leader. He's a novelist, apparently, and when he discovered that Earth had a thriving publishing industry... Well, he wanted in on the action. Anyway, have you read it?"

Fletcher stared at MS. He frowned. "Skimmed. And..."

"Yes?"

"Well... to be honest, it's not very good. And way too long."

"When has quality ever stood in the way of your purchasing a title, Fletch?"

"Point taken. But I mean to say, this is really bad. And I'm not just talking Dan Brown bad, or even pop-star-writes-his-own-memoirs bad. Of course, that isn't a major problem. Now, if it were half the current length..."

"Sorted, Fletch. I've already got Hemmings on the job. You'll be the first to put an alien novel on the market."

He thought about it. "So… What are we talking, here?" he said, getting down to the nitty-gritty.

"I want quarter of a million, plus ten per cent royalties. We can talk about the fine detail over lunch."

"I'll have to put it to marketing, of course."

Fletcher's title might have been commissioning editor, but we all knew who did the commissioning these days.

I said, "Pronto, old boy? I mean, if you do want lunch today...? The Ivy. On me."

He put a call through to marketing, outlining the deal.

Five minutes later a bright young thing from marketing, leggy, blonde and about thirteen years old, burst into the room high on gush.

She came bounding over and gripped my hand. "William Carstairs? I'm Fizz. I'll be handling the project. Must say, we're all really really excited. And honoured, of course. Honoured to be handling the work of such a galactically recognised author. And I'm told the novel's really really super-good."

"Super-good," I said.

"It's just a pity the alien isn't more... photogenic, yeah?"

"You mean, sexy?"

"Well, you must admit..." She gestured to the Daily Mail on Fletcher's desk. The front page carried a colour photo of Glag meeting the PM. The blue alien octopus was even uglier than the Terran version. And even uglier than the PM, which was going some.

I patted Fizz's pretty little head. "I'm confident the boys and girls in marketing will find an angle..."

She was oblivious to my irony.

"You bet, William. We're working on it, like, now." Fizz wrinkled her nose, waggled fingers and hurried from the office.

Fletcher clapped his hands. "Done deal. Did you say the Ivy?"

The next few days were hectic. I made sure all the press had the gen and arranged for Glag to go on a publicity tour.

The alien went down a storm on national TV. He proved a wise and witty raconteur, with a penchant for fine champagne.

I stood behind the cameras as Ross interviewed the tentacled Glag.

"Now, I've read your novel and I think it's a blinder! How do you think it'll go down on planet Earth?"

Glag's response was a series of glottal plosives which sounded as if he were gargling with liquidized frogs. The silver box, floating beside its head, duly translated, "I think it will have the effect of opening your minds to the fact of life on other planets."

Ross clapped. "I'm sure it will, Glag. Now, reassure me that you're not here to eat us!"

"Eat you?" Glag responded. "What an appalling thought! We are a peaceable people, Jonathon!" It raised three champagne glasses and slurped.

Ross clapped Glag on a tentacle. "Only kidding! I can't tell you how thrilled I am at having you on the show. Ladies and gentlemen, give it up for Glag!"

The day of publication fast approached, just a month after I sealed the deal with Greenwood and Worley.

An initial print run of twenty-five million copies was printed and stored under lock and key in an East End warehouse. Armed guards patrolled the perimeter. Midnight deliveries to all major supermarkets and bookshops ensured an eager public would be supplied with copies at extraordinary dawn openings.

I lined up a launch party at the Savoy and made sure the BBC were on hand to record the event.

We'd mocked up a facsimile Betelgeusian ship and, amid a suitably alien fanfare and much liquid nitrogen swamp-effects, Glag emerged down the ramp clutching a copy of his magnum opus, the first alien novel ever to be published on Earth.

A queue of over a thousand eager citizens clamoured for Glag's singular moniker. Fortunately he possessed eight pseudopods and his signature consisted of the briefest of squiggles.

Towards midnight, as the hordes of satisfied customers had departed and the party was winding down, I split a celebratory bottle of red with Hemmings.

The author, pouch-eyed and pale-faced after the speedy shortening of Glag's novel, leaned towards me and slurred, "Had a word with Fizz."

"Mmm?" I was watching Glag and Fletcher across the room. There seemed to be some altercation in progress, which occasioned an unseemly writhing of multiple extraterrestrial pseudopods.

"Fizz!" Hemmings reiterated. "Blonde schoolgirl who runs Greenwood and Worley these days."

"And?" I was still distracted. Glag was turning an odd shade of puce and waving a copy of its novel in a threatening manner.

"Fizz told me what the bastards paid you. A quarter of a million sodding pounds. And you gave me… What was it, a measly ten grand? And what did the alien get, Carstairs?

"That's between me and my client."

"But ten measly thousand quid! And no royalties!"

Oh, how I despair of moaning authors! "That was the offer on the table, Hemmings. I seem to recall you almost snapped my hand off."

He slumped back into his seat, drooling saliva and wine. "See you in court, Carstairs, you robbing bastard!"

"Excuse me one moment, Hemmings. Fletcher seems to be in trouble..."

The sozzled scribe grunted a laugh as I hurried across the room to Fletcher's aid.

Glag was multi-tasking: two pseudopods were flicking through the pages of its novel while a further pair were gripping Fletcher's torso. The remaining four suckered tentacles whisked around its head in angry semaphore.

"Ah… what seems to be the problem?" I said.

Fletcher managed a strangulated, "He's…*erk*… read the novel–"

Glag gurgled and the silver box translated, "Your excisions have rendered it a travesty of my heart-felt prose, sirs. A traducing of my lofty sentiments. A trivialisation of my intellectual ideals held in great esteem by my people! I wil l–" and here the translator merely regurgitated what sounded like 'splurch' "– splurch the being responsible for this." Glag raised six tentacles, menacingly, above Fletcher's head. "This might occasion a diplomatic rift between our planets, but –"

"One moment!" I cried. "Mr Fletcher is an entirely innocent party in all this, Glag. The guilty party, who made the cuts..." And I indicated the semi-comatose Hemmings across the room.

"He was responsible?" said Glag.

"And he alone…"

Glag un-tentacled Fletcher, rose to its full height of some eight feet, and ambulated itself in fluid motion across the floor, homing in on the hapless Hemmings.

I took the opportunity to slip quickly from the Savoy, wondering, as I did so, what Glag meant by *splotchy*...

From the sounds issuing from within the building, and from Hemmings' throat specifically, it didn't sound all that pleasant.

*Three: Glag*

The invasion was going swimmingly until I discovered what they had done to my novel and I splurched the writerly human.

I really should have restrained myself. By splurching the writer, I might easily have given the game away.

I stared down at his writhing somaform, wondering how I might retrieve the situation. Fortunately, the room was emptying and only Fletcher the Publisher was aware of what I had done. He was staring across at me, an odd expression on his large, red face.

This gave me an idea.

I left the human gurbling with the ghorks, hurried across to the trembling publisher and gripped him in four tentacles. He trembled and stared up at me in fear.

I said, "I demanded reparations, Fletcher!"

"Ah… reparations?"

"Do you see Hemmings the Writer?"

He looked across the room, aghast, and nodded.

"I take it you would like to be spared a similar fate?"

Gagging, he merely nodded.

"Then accede to these demands: the pulping forthwith of all copies of my novel and the speedy publication of said novel in its original and uncut form. Do you agree?"

Fletcher moved his head up and down. "Yes. Yes, of course!"

I released him and he slumped to the floor, weeping.

"I will be in touch," I said, and exited the building full of foreboding. It was but a short taxi ride to Hyde Park where my ship sat, a reassuring bulk against the night sky.

I retired to my hibernation pod and slept for a day. Splurching always has that effect on me.

When I awoke, I poured myself seven glasses of restorative champagne and called an emergency meeting with my compatriots, world-wide.

When all five hundred of my fellow Jesta-puxa'telepalational-ixajesima-nagorational-aspatorians were virtually convened in my quarters, I gave them the news.

"The first phase of our plans has been thwarted by the humans," I began, waving my free tentacle in consternation.

"But the scheme was fool-proof," said Glit, my Paris representative.

"So I thought, but I reckoned without the scribes of Earth. A particular human called Hemmings excised the text, so scrambling the embedded Subliminal Code of Submission."

"But how did he know?"

"I suspect he didn't. He made the cuts in a bid to make the text more acceptable to the average low intelligence of the humans."

Glit raised four tentacles in a gesture of consternation. "But I thought the Cognational Blocking Beam should have prevented such tampering."

I waved a tentacle in admission of dereliction. "I instituted the CBB in order to prevent the humans *rewriting* the text. Little did I realise that they might cut my hallowed prose."

Glit said, "So how do we proceed?"

I informed my compatriots of the agreement I had elicited from Fletcher the Publisher.

Gulk, in New York, asked, "But can Fletcher the Publisher be trusted to keep his word?"

"That is my deepest worry, of course. The humans are a duplicitous race. And my cortical-scans of Fletcher show that he is a most unreliable individual."

Glit raised four tentacles in a gesture of consternation. "It is imperative that the text is published without adulteration!"

I retreated into a mood of lugubrious funk, wondering if I had done the wise thing in threatening Fletcher with splurching.

An aide hurried into my quarters. "Sir! A delegation of humans is demanding an audience!"

I drained the remaining champagne and made my way to the top of the ramp.

A quartet of humans arrayed itself outside the ship.

I made out the human called Carstairs the Literary Agent. Beside him was Fletcher the Publisher. To the fore, and pushing a wheelchair, was the child I had met at the publishing house, whose influence, I gleaned, was out of all proportion to her meagre years. Fizz, her name.

Her soft pink face was set in lines I translated as denoting indignation, as she propelled the wheelchair up the ramp.

In the wheelchair was the human known as Hemmings the Writer, though he no longer resembled the human known as Hemmings the Writer.

"I don't know what you did to poor Richard," Fizz said as she stormed aboard. "But I want it undone, now!"

Carstairs and Fletcher, cowering, crept into the ship in her wake. "I don't think this is at all wise," Fletcher murmured to the child.

"Oh, shut up, can't you? I dragged you along for some moral support! They're squid, for chrissake! What can they do to us?"

"Ah..." said the one known as Carstairs, "splurch us, Fizz?"

She propelled Hemmings before me and demanded, "Glag, de-splurch him this very minute!"

I considered the child; she appeared brave beyond her years, in complete contrast to the middle-aged human ducking and bobbing in mortal fear behind her.

I had an idea.

I could use a creature as resourceful and resolute as Fizz.

"De-splurching is... possible, Fizz. But let me tell you that it is a highly complex and risky manoeuvre. If I were to consent to accede to your desires, there would be a condition."

She struck a pose wholly meaningless to me: head cocked to one side, fist lodged on jutting hip. "Name it."

"If I were to de-splurch Hemmings, restore him to his erstwhile state, then you must agree to work for... no, alongside... me."

She made an odd shape with her lips, like one of the human's grammatical commas, only much larger. "What exactly would that consist of, Glag? And what's in it for me, like, euro-wise?"

I leaned forward, whispered in her ear, and watched her face transform itself. Her lips became much longer and she exhibited an increased expanse of dental enamel. "Glag, you've got yourself a deal!"

I positioned myself before the wheelchair-bound Hemmings, raised the requisite six tentacles, inflated my de-venom sacks, and commenced the lengthy process of de-splurching the writer.

Fifteen minutes later the grey scales of fungus fell from his body, ghork grubs worked themselves out of his epidermis, and his cognitive functions returned to normal. He fell into Fizz's arms, weeping.

Fizz winked at me. "I'll be in touch, Glag." She turned to the pusillanimous human. "Fletcher, Carstairs, come here and help me with Hemmings!"

My story is almost over.

The invasion of Earth approaches completion.

Over the past month a billion copies of my novel, uncut, have been snapped up by voracious readers – and that was merely the English version. Fizz oversaw the publication and sale of the novel in a further one hundred and fifty languages. I estimate that ninety-five per cent of the citizens on the planet have read my book – which is sufficient for our purposes.

I spoke with Fizz this morning.

The screen showed me the scene inside her Hampstead apartment. I made out Hemmings in one corner, tapping away at a PC.

Fizz said, "He was ever so grateful for what I did, yeah? Me and him, we're like this, now." And she made a small gesture with two of her digits. "He's writing an account of his splurching. Apparently, he hallucinated he was on an alien planet, being consumed by… *icky* things."

Hallucinated, I thought to myself, chortling. "Hemmings is a very lucky man, Fizz."

Typically of her, she took this solipsistically. "Thanks, Glag!"

"But to other things... I take it that all is prepared?"

"Abso-cool-lutely, Glag!" Fizz carolled. "I've co-ordinated a, like, super-massive advertising campaign. We've read the novel – now we want to experience the reality!"

"So phase two can proceed?"

"Roll 'em on!"

I waved tentacles in anticipatory delight, thanked my Earthside management co-ordinator, and signed off.

What we didn't tell the people of Earth, of course, was the real reason we came to their planet.

My homeworld is terribly overcrowded, and Earth is perfect for our requirements.

Overnight, my fleet of starships disgorged millions of Body Booths in cities, towns and villages across the face of the world. Soon, primed by the subliminal codes embedded in my novel, the humans will be lining up outside the booths in their millions for the once in a lifetime opportunity to experience life on other worlds...

My fellow Jesta-puxa'telepalational-ixajesima-nagorational-aspatorians are experts in overseeing the process of mind-transference – otherwise known as splurching.

But we are not merciless invaders: we think the humans will be perfectly content in the bodies of Denebian sludge-hogs. And the bodies they leave behind in our aptly named Body Booths will be quickly and efficiently incinerated.

Incinerated – not, as I made clear to the execrable Ross, *eaten.*

But not all the humans will be transferred, I have decided. The champagne makers of France, for instance, will continue to produce their heavenly nectar. And in gratitude for her inestimable hard work on our behalf, I will spare Fizz and her mate, Hemmings the Writer.

The pair will, I think, make fascinating pets.

# The Rest is Speculation

*I have no idea where this strange vision came from, nor the origins of the idea. It was one of those happy notions that pop into the mind of a writer from time to time – but not often, more's the pity. Most tales have to be thought about for a long time, then worked at to get the plot, and then rewritten again and again. This came in a spurt, wrote itself, and aside from quite a bit of pruning didn't need that much work. I do recall that the initial image was of the cliff-side city and the waterless sea-bed, and that the first paragraph extended for more than a page, before the necessary excision.*

The dead city thrust itself from the escarpment above the vanished sea, its soaring towers and minarets a lament in stone for the race that aeons past had lifted it, block by block, towards the heavens. Something about its vaulting design might have inspired awe long ago, but now evoked mere sadness. And the great scoop of the drained ocean, which fell away from the city to a desiccated sea-bed split by chasms and fissures miles below, was just as monumentally tragic.

I know that I was born and that I died, but the rest is speculation. My death I recall but dimly: my passing had an odd elusive sense of déjà-vu, as if I had been travelling towards this familiar place all my life. I was surrounded by loved ones, I think, and I was not in pain; death was a sadness, not so much a longing for more but a desire to have it all again; death was a diminishing of the senses, a dwindling towards a beckoning darkness.

And then came the light.

"Where am I?"

After my initial panic and confusion I was flooded by a sense of calm.

"Be easy. You are well. We welcome you."

I was in a vast chamber seared with sunlight that fell *en bloc* from a far window, and an odd creature confronted me.

"You are," I said, "a crab."

The crab waved one of its of four large pincers, as if conducting an orchestra. "I am a member of the race known as the Ky[20], and my name is Replenish-362."

"And my name," I said, as if constrained by a reciprocal formality, "is..." But for the life of me I could not recall my name.

"It is of little matter," said Replenish-362. The words came from a small silver box slung beneath the chitinous letter-box of its unmoving mouth. I too wore a similar device about my neck. "You may call me Rep. I will call you… Channon, I think."

"Channon…" I repeated. I knew I was not dreaming: the experience had the clarity of reality.

"Rep," I said, "what am I doing here?"

"In time," said Rep. "In time."

"But am I on Earth?" I persisted.

Rep waved a pincer. "You are on Earth."

Then I noticed we were not alone.

A figure vaguely human-shaped stood behind Rep, and a little to one side. It was twice as tall as an average human, and silver, and across the surface of its face passed a series of evanescent features, as if it were cycling through a sequential amalgam of every human face that had ever been. I did not know whether this being was male or female, but from it I sensed an emanation of such peace and tranquillity that I almost wept.

"I am Kamis," said the silver being. "Or, rather, that is the name given me by Rep." Its lips moved, but out of synchronisation with its words, which issued instead from its own silver box. "I am from the race which translates in your language as the shimmer-folk."

Then the ceiling moved, or so I thought. Startled, I stared up (only then realising that I lay on a surface canted at a forty-five degree angle) and saw that what descended was not the ceiling but another creature, this one like a manta ray, a flat golden hovering thing with four eyes set in its underside between an array of waving cilia.

"And Rep calls me Cheth," said the ray, "of the villicent people. I greet you, Channon."

As it lowered itself and levitated beside Kamis, I saw that the creature called Cheth was perhaps five metres broad, and as many long.

I leaned forward, and the surface on which I rested tipped me to my feet. I stood with surprise, and another surprise awaited me as I looked down the length of my naked body. Dimly I recalled my former body, but gone was the stringy, wasted, pain-wracked frame of old. I seemed forty again, trim and well-muscled.

I looked at the three very different creatures before me and said, "Where am I? How did I get here?"

"You are," said Replenish-362, "in the year two billion, four hundred and five million, three hundred and fifty-five thousand, two hundred and twenty-three, by your reckoning of these things."

"Two billion…" I began.

Kamis inclined its silver head, and I saw a procession of smiles decorate its face "Give or take several hundred million years," it said.

"But how…?" I gestured towards the chamber, the sunlight behind the trio.

Rep stepped forward, legs ticking upon the floor. "You would not understand the science of the process, Channon," it said. "Suffice to say that we accessed your DNA-identity, and enabled you, and brought you to fruition."

Kamis gestured with a silver hand. "Just as my identity was accessed, and enabled, and brought to fruition. I too am like you, though from an age long after yours. Almost ten million years after, which itself seen from this age seems ancient history indeed."

Rep said, "Cheth hails from a more recent age."

The manta ray spoke. "I am from Earth of just three million, five hundred thousand years ago. We were the dominant species on the planet for almost four million years, and that time was a time of peace and prosperity, of learning and high culture. It ended," Cheth went on, "it ended, as all things must do."

"Four million years," I said. Then, "And do you know how long *Homo sapiens* walked the planet?"

"From the time when you began to keep records," Rep said, "to your extinction, was but four hundred thousand years."

"Which," said Kamis, "might seem a long time, but is just an eye-blink in the long history of our planet. My people had records of your reign on Earth. You were, if you will pardon me, a primitive species. You… fought, waged war, despoiled the Earth."

"But," Rep put in, "too they were inventive, and artistic, and philosophically inclined."

"That I acknowledge," Kamis said, inclining its argent head.

I smiled. "I have little memory of who I was, of who my people were."

Kamis said, "Cheth and I, too, came to fruition with little knowledge of our identities, our histories."

"You underwent," Rep said, "extensive trauma in being enabled; of course you will experience certain… shall we say… cognitive dysfunctions, for a time."

I looked at the crab-like being. "And can you tell me why I was accessed, enabled, and brought to fruition?"

The crab did a little dance, or what looked like a dance; a quick skittering jig with much chitinous tattooing on the marble floor. Quickly, without replying, it moved around the surface on which I had lain and tip-toed towards an aperture which slid open upon its approach.

"Kamis, Cheth," it called.

The two creatures complied, moving towards the door. Cheth said, "Rep will not impart the reason for our arrival in this age, my friend. It says, 'In time, in time'."

They joined Rep, who swivelled and said to me, "In one hour we begin our journey, Channon. Your provisions will be brought. Until then…" It gestured with a pincer, then left the chamber with Kamis and Cheth.

I stood, alone, bathed in sunlight.

I moved towards a vast window which bulged out from the room. I saw the great mountain range on either hand, serried peaks falling gradually towards what I guessed to be a dried up sea-bed. I later learned that I was right; that once this was indeed a mighty ocean. The seabed was silver and split with deep, dark fissures.

I stopped at the edge of the room, where the marble tiles segued seamlessly into the transparent material of the window.

I gasped, for a city fell away at my feet. It was as if I were levitating in the air, and was gazing upon a series of alleys and stairways as they fell down the shelving slope of the mountainside. I saw buildings like beehives, and towers which speared past where I stood, and a million windows looking out over the desiccated seabed – but I beheld not a single figure in all the sprawling, falling cityscape, not one being to suggest that this perpendicular metropolis harboured life. It seemed as dead as the silver, dried up seabed far below.

Then I looked up and saw the sun, and I almost sobbed.

It filled the breadth of the horizon, and was bisected by that far away line of land, a great red fulminating dome that pulsed with life – or rather a semblance of life: magnificent molten eject, spuming geysers, looping strands of liquid fire. I laughed in awe at the sight, and knew it for the most wondrous thing I had ever witnessed.

I heard a sound behind me and turned quickly.

In the centre of the chamber a pile of clothing and what looked like a stylised backpack now reposed upon a silver disc, where nothing had stood before,

I left the window to inspect these things – the provisions, no doubt, which Rep had promised.

The clothing comprised a silver suit fashioned from a material so soft and light that I stood fondling it for minutes, smiling in wonder. The backpack was of a like material, and contained canisters holding what I guessed might be water. There were other objects in the pack: something like a pen, which I could not work, and a silver ball which defied my comprehension.

I pulled on the one-piece overall, which quickly shrank to hug my body and head, with a diaphanous membrane before my face. I looked up, attracted by something, and made out hovering above my head what looked like a halo; I smiled at the thought.

Rep had mentioned a journey; and was I now fully equipped? My curiosity was piqued. A journey, presumably, outside, in that harsh and sun-scorched landscape? And for what purpose? And this, in turn, brought my thoughts to the reason for my… what had Rep called it… my fruition? At any rate, my presence in this wondrous age?

I shook my head and moved, as if compelled, towards the bulging window again, and stared out at the ancient Earth tortured by the engorged sun, and wondered what awaited me out there.

The aperture swished open and Rep jigged in on tip-toe, followed by the tall and striding Kamis; behind them, Cheth furled its wings to accommodate its passage into the chamber.

Rep said, "Ah, I see you have prepared yourself."

"For what, I would like to know," I said.

"For a journey to the end of the Earth," Rep said, "with many a wonder upon the way."

"Which," said Kamis with a hint of humour, "is as much as our crustacean friend has deigned to tell us, despite our constant questions."

"How long have you both been… enabled?" I asked.

The giant manta-ray known as Cheth replied, "Two days, no more."

"A day for me," answered Kamis. "A day of wonders enough, without promise of more."

Rep was leading the way towards the bulging window; we followed. As the crab-being approached, the transparent material opened like a clam-shell, hinged up to give access to a precipitous flight of stairs wide enough to accommodate even Cheth. I followed Rep, with Kamis by my side and Cheth bringing up the rear.

I had expected fierce heat, a searing wind. The reality was that the atmosphere without differed not in the slightest from that within the chamber. I breathed cool air, was aware of no hot wind.

We moved down the stairs away from the jutting chamber.

Ahead, as if discerning my puzzlement, Rep twisted an eye-stalk and regarded me with a black orb. It said, "The suit you wear is equipped to equalise the temperature, to shield you from the worst of this world's inclemencies."

I pointed. "And the halo?"

"You might call it a… a solar panel," Rep said, "or at least a solar collector. At any rate, it gives power to your suit."

I looked at Kamis. "You wear no suit…" I began.

Something like a million different smiles chased themselves across the creature's face. "In my time the sun, though not this size, was almost beyond the tolerance of most living creatures. We adapted, suited our forms to the solar radiation."

"And you, Cheth?" I asked.

"Likewise," it replied. "My tegument is adapted, armoured. I use to my advantage that which many creatures would find inimical."

I smiled. "I am a primitive indeed," I said.

The humane Kamis said, "The happenstance of your genealogy does not preclude your potentiality, my friend."

I smiled and nodded and gave my attention to the descent.

I guessed that the city was not built by human beings, or rather by any human beings that might have conformed to my approximate dimensions. For one thing the steps were too high, suggesting architects with longer legs than mine; for another, the apertures leading from the steps to the dwellings on either side were tall and attenuated: I would have had to turn sideways to gain entry. I imagined a city peopled by a race of thin, long-legged giants.

Seconds later I heard a distant rumble, followed by a tremor; I staggered. It was as if for an instant my legs had turned to jelly.

Rep explained, "The Earth is old, and suffers quakes from time to time."

Kamis, beside me, asked Rep, "And this city? Is it a redundancy to ask if it is no longer inhabited?"

"The last guardians left its shelter and took refuge underground some half a million years gone," Rep said. "They became extinct long ago."

"Guardians? But they were not the beings who built the city?" Cheth asked.

"No. The last inhabitants were spider creatures, living here like vermin and hardly sentient, we think."

"But do you know who did build the city?" I asked.

"A race known as the Effectuators," Rep told us. "They were a hallowed people, a philosopher race. Their artefacts can be found all over the surface of this old planet."

"And the stars," I said to myself. "In two billions years, the stars would have been conquered."

"Legions of races have left the refuge of planet Earth and gone among the stars, in search of knowledge and wisdom, adventure. And aliens," Rep went on, "stop by from time to time, with stories of their wanderings, and even tales of the many Terran races they have happened upon out there."

"And you?" Kamis asked. "Are your people, the $Ky^{20}$, a star-faring race?"

Replenish-362 raised two pincers in an indecipherable gesture. "We have never left the cradle of our birth, my friend. We leave adventuring to more daring species."

Cheth asked, "If this, then, is not your city – where do you dwell?"

"We are a subterranean species," Rep replied. "We live in vast excavated caverns in the cool far underground."

"But what," I said, "is the reason for your venturing out on this quest, if I might ask?"

The crab waved four pincers. "That will become apparent in time, in time."

Beside me, Kamis smiled.

We had passed through a series of shelved dwellings, and now approached an escarpment. To either side were terraced ellipses, which once, in far earlier times, might have been gardens. Now they were parched furrows, from which even the soil had been dried to dust and stolen by the wind.

We stopped before what appeared to be a sheer drop, and Rep gestured with its largest pincer. "Behold."

The dehydrated seabed stretched away before us like some lifeless lunar landscape, magnificent not only in its size but in its silence, its grandeur made all the more impressive by the backdrop of the apoplectic sun.

At first I thought its only features the cracks and rills that striated its surface; but then I made out tiny specks of wrecked vessels canted and embedded in the silt, and here and there scattered about the shattered plain I glimpsed what might once have been former dwellings, agglomerations of bubble-domes and things like termite mounds, cracked and crumbled now. The landscape was as bereft of colour as of life: a dozen shades of grey predominated, from dull pewter to silver. I looked about for signs of vegetation, but saw only sporadic, stunted bind-weed, ground hugging and the colour of straw.

Indeed the only real colour provided was the bloody hue of the sun, which filled the air with a light like wine.

Rep gestured towards the ruined domes. "Long ago the Kleem took to the sea, and became in time aquatic. They raised great submarine cities, and for aeons were the dominant species on the planet. Their days passed, however, and their cities fell to ruin."

"When did this race prosper?" I asked.

"The Kleem were relatively recent, approximately nine million years gone. Some say they went to the stars aboard vast water-filled arks, when the seas of Earth began to dry, but that is only apocryphal."

We were standing on an apron of stone jutting out above the canyon, and I could see no steps leading the rest of the way.

Kamis said, "We will cross the bottom of this vanished sea?"

"We will," Rep answered.

"I see no means of descent," I said.

Rep waved a humorous pincer. "Our means is amongst us," it said, and gestured towards Cheth.

The manta ray being descended and prostrated itself across the sun-blasted stones, like some vast and living mat of silver. "Step aboard," it said, voice muffled.

I glanced at Kamis, who gestured that I should go first.

Rep said, "Move to the middle and be seated. I assure you that you will be safe."

"And I second that assurance," came the modulated response from the ray's hidden mouth.

Tentatively, I took a step, and then another, across the flesh of the being, which gave beneath my tread like the surface of a liverish trampoline. I expected cries of surprise or pain from my host, but it was silent as I lowered myself and sat cross-legged on the broad back. I reached out and felt its skin: it was cold and rough, like frozen sand-paper.

Kamis sat beside me and Rep took up position ahead of us, eye-stalks peering forward as we lifted and floated out over the void.

This was what I imagined riding a flying carpet must be like. Cheth moved slowly at first, the edges of its wings scrolled to ensure our safety. There was no sensation of vertigo – the extent of Cheth's back was such that we had no sheer vision of the drop beneath us – or even danger; what I felt was a heady exhilaration as we picked up speed and descended in a great swooping parabola towards the seabed.

I looked up and back, and saw the city move away from us with surprising speed. It presented an aged face, blasted by the sun, and I wondered how mighty it had been aeons ago, fully populated by its builders, abustle with life unimaginable to me. I looked ahead and wondered at our destination.

I was skewered then by a fierce lancing stab of regret, and I tried to locate its source. I sensed the feelings I had felt for… loved ones, and I knew that much of the joy of my previous life, so long ago, had been due to my shared experiences with them. How much more, I felt, I would appreciate what was happening now if only these faceless, nameless people were by my side to share this wondrous ride.

I tried to recapture lost memories, but experienced only abstractions, wellings of love as evanescent as lost dreams, and no more.

At one point we were side-swiped by a fierce wind, and rocked a little, and Kamis reached out with a silver hand and steadied me. The touch was a revelation. Whatever I had expected, it was not this: that its touch should communicate the essence of its humanity – a feeble word to use of a being not even human. It was as if Kamis had communicated directly with my brain, as if its touch was all I needed to know that Kamis was good.

In time we came to the surface of the seabed, and hovered along perhaps two metres above the drifted silver sands. We passed close by the shattered domes, among which stood monuments of the Kleem – their great and good, no doubt – with wasted bodies and bulbous heads, and fins instead of limbs. There was something ineffably sad about the ruins, the canted broken statues and the domes half-buried in scintillating drifts, as if we were passing through not the remains of a city but a graveyard. Indeed, I thought, that was what planet Earth had become in this advanced age two billion years from my own time, an august graveyard of the many races that had lived and died in ignorance of what might succeed them.

It was a sobering thought as we left behind the once-submarine city and headed towards the roiling hemisphere of the swollen sun.

"Does the sun ever set?" I asked.

Rep said, "The rotation of planet Earth has slowed considerably over the millennia. A day now lasts almost a week, in your reckoning; a year lasts five of your years. The seasons are correspondingly protracted. We are in winter now."

"Winter?" Kamis said, surprised. "If this is winter, then what must summer be like?"

"A time of solar storms when the surface of the planet is

uninhabitable, and all creatures burrow deep underground. A minute on the surface in high summer spells certain death."

"So that is why," said Cheth beneath us, "we are making this voyage now, in winter?"

Rep inclined an eye-stalk. "That is why indeed."

The silence stretched as we waited for Rep to continue; it deigned not to, and we did not press it.

Beside me, Kamis raised a hand and touched its temple. I said, "You are in pain?"

"Not pain," it said, a smile racing across its varied features. "I had a sudden… a fleeting return of memory. And yet... the memory is vague, though hauntingly strong, if that is not a contradiction. I recall a time in my childhood, when I accompanied my clan on a pilgrimage to the sea. It was the annual time of rejoicing in the fecundity of nature."

"Tell us," said Cheth.

The tall silver man sat up straight and looked ahead, into the sun. "There is little to tell, sadly. I recall great happiness, and safety. I was with my siblings, all thirty-odd of them, and we knew with the certainty of youth that the future held wondrous and miraculous events in store for us. I... I can sense more, feelings of tragedy, of elation, but it is as if these might belong to another person, so nebulous are they." It paused, then said, "And you, Cheth? What do you recall?"

The manta ray replied, "Like you, my recollections are vague, abstract. As to specific instances of my life – these I find impossible to place, to pin down." It stopped there, then continued, "I receive the impression that we were like creatures in a small pond, which dreamed of the life that might exist out there, but which could only think within the narrow remit of the pond containing us." It paused, then said, "And you, Channon?"

I shook my head. "I have no recollections, other than maddening abstractions. I do know that those of my race were short-lived compared to yourselves. We lived perhaps seventy, eighty, ninety years in total."

"So little time!" Rep said, aghast.

"No time," Kamis went on, "to assess one's suitability for… for *anything*."

I smiled. "In retrospect, I think we humans spent so much time mired in regret, wishing things were… different. Perhaps that's the corollary of living such short lives."

I considered my words, then said tentatively, "Kamis, Cheth, do either of you recall loved ones, family?"

A silence greeted my words, and then Kamis said, "I recall lovers… I think. In a lifetime of a thousand years, we would have perhaps thirty or forty partners, often concurrently. But the depth of our love for each other was not diminished by this fact. And yet…" A frown chased itself across its shimmering face. "And yet I recall no specific mates."

"Cheth?" I asked.

"Unlike the shimmer-folk, we villicents had but one lover in a lifetime, to whom we were devoted until death. But for the life of me, sadly, I do not recall the specifics of a mate."

A silence fell. Were we three thinking the same thing? That this absence, this lacunae in our memories, was a common link between us.

We rode on.

Perhaps an hour passed before Rep said, "I think the time has arrived to pause for refreshments."

Duly Cheth slowed and came to rest a foot above the silver sands. We stepped off, into hot silt that lapped about our ankles, and Cheth rose so that it could regard us with the eyes which adorned its underside.

From our backpacks we took the canisters, all except Cheth, who was without provisions.At my enquiry it explained, "The sunlight is enough, my friend, to provide all my bodily needs."

I watched Rep as it deftly unscrewed the lid from a canister and tipped it towards its letter-box mouth. A foamy liquid poured out. Kamis, tentatively, did likewise, then nodded. "Quite wonderful," it opined.

"A nutrient which will provide you with strength," Rep said.

I opened my canister and drank. The liquid frothed and spangled upon my palate, leaving me feeling both refreshed and satisfied.

"And these?" I asked, taking out the silver ball and the pencil-like implement.

"The sphere is a protector," Rep said. "It maintains a field about your person which repels any predators that might be lurking."

"Predators?"

"Strange beasts patrol the torrid wastes," Rep said.

"And the sticks?" Kamis asked.

"Keys," said Rep.

A silence, then we all three asked in concert, "Keys, for what?"

Rep's eye-stalks moved from Kamis to Cheth to me. "For what comes next, my friends," it said with maddening taciturnity.

"And that might be?" I ventured.

Its eye-stalks swivelled until they were regarding the sun. It gestured with a pincer and said, "Look, our bellicose primary has loosed a supra-flare."

We looked, and beheld, emerging from the bloated belly of the sun, a quick lick of flame racing through space towards the planet.

"But what," said Cheth, "has this to do with the keys we carry?"

"In time, in time," said the damnable crab. "Follow me. The flare will arrive in perhaps one hour, and it would be well if we were far below the surface when it blasts the land."

Rep minced towards an outcropping of rock, and we followed.

As it approached what appeared to be a slab of fractured basalt, a circular aperture in the flank of the rock irised to reveal a hovering disk of flat metal, perhaps five metres across. Rep stepped onto the disk, and we joined it. Instantly we were aboard, the disk dropped. I cried out in consternation and reached out to Kamis, who steadied me. The hovering Cheth gave a cry of surprise and dropped with us.

A minute later the disk slowed its rapid descent, and I stepped off it into a chamber which staggered my senses with its dimensions.

The chamber was v-shaped, perhaps a hundred metres tall, constructed of some brilliant white ceramic substance, and it diminished into the distance for as far as the eye could see. Its sloping sides were scored with galleries, and on the ground-floor and on each gallery – and I counted twenty of them before the distance defeated my eyesight – dozens of crabs like Replenish-362 worked at banks of consoles.

Their activity was frantic as they skittered back and forth, tapping at surfaces, adjusting panels, conferring together and then parting in great haste.

Kamis voiced what I was thinking, "What is happening here?"

"These are scientists," Rep said. "They are carrying out the work of the Effectuators."

"What work? Kamis asked.

The reticent crab kept its own counsel and its eye-stalks peered ahead as it led us along the chamber.

I recalled mention of the keys. "Our keys have some function down here?" I asked as we pursued the skittering crab.

We came to a canted series of consoles, etched with arcane hieroglyphs and indented with several slots. At the sight of us, three crabs working at the consoles backed off, eyes-stalks turned our way, and watched us as we approached with Rep.

"If each of you takes a console, and inserts the key into the appropriate aperture..."

Hastily, Kamis and I unfastened our packs and withdrew the pen-like implement. Rep stirred a pincer in its own pack, and withdrew a stick which it passed to Cheth, who manoeuvred its cilia to accept it.

I stepped forward, towards the console, and slipped the pen point first into the appropriate slot. It was tugged from my grip in a rush… and I have no explanation for what happened next.

It was as if the chamber ceased to exist. I was in a white limitless area, and out of the opalescence which surrounded me coalesced a series of images, a rapid procession of incidents which I knew – somehow – to be the history of planet Earth.

And then I beheld a hundred creatures, a thousand, and with each one I was granted its name, its place in history, its significance. And I knew the planet Earth to be a wondrous place which over billions of years had played host to all manner of sentient lifeforms, races and species which had spanned hundreds of thousands of years before passing into oblivion, or a million years before disappearing from evolution's stage: but whatever the race, and however long they ruled the planet, their fate was certain: they would one day hand the flame of the planet's stewardship on to another emergent race.

And then I was looking upon a creature I knew, somehow, to be an Effectuator: a bipedal ant-like being with a human's swollen cranium. It turned and regarded me, and then smiled, and an exquisite sensation of well-being flooded my senses. I had the sudden knowledge, then, as it peered at me, that I was being assessed by this being, judged even, but for what I could not guess.

I had a dozen questions, more, but at that instant I was whisked from the opalescent realm and I found myself back in the chamber surrounded by the scurrying crabs, with Kamis and Cheth by my side and Rep standing before me, regarding us with its eye-stalks.

Kamis was the first to gather its thoughts, and I knew from what it said that it had experienced much the same as I. "And what," it said, "became of the Effectuators?"

Rep said, "They… ascended, stepped up, and employed us, the humble species known as Ky[20], to do their bidding."

"Which is?" Kamis said.

"And what," I asked, "do they want with us? I felt I was being… *judged* – but for what?"

Instead of replying, Rep moved away from the consoles, back towards the aperture which housed the elevator disc. It stepped upon it, and we had little option but to follow.

Rep was silent as we rode to the surface of the planet and stepped out into the scorched landscape.

Much was as it had been, but for twists and torques of fire scattered about the sea-bed, combustible material ignited by the errant supra-flare.

Rep gestured, and Cheth descended. We accommodated ourselves upon its back, and the manta rose and flew towards the sun.

We travelled for hours, and the sun expanded to fill fully half the sky. I dozed, and dreamed, lucid images of men and women, golden humans who radiated greatness, and I was filled by an inexpressible surge of joy, of ineffable rapture. The intensity was such that it brought me awake, and for seconds I was disconcerted to find myself riding upon the back of a strange creature, across a dying Earth, towards a boiling sun.

I closed my eyes and attempted to recapture the images, to access memories so far denied me. I failed to recall specific instances of my life before, but I did come upon nebulous feelings, maddeningly elusive: feelings of love and hope, upwellings of basic emotion. They were so general they might have belonged to any human at any time in history.

We were travelling high above a seabed obscured by drifting sands. I thought I saw, to my left, a mountainside shiver and collapse. I blinked, and the movement of my travelling companions, as they turned and watched the looming peak crumble and slide into the seabed, alerted me to the fact that I was not hallucinating.

"What is happening?" asked Kamis.

"The Earth," Rep replied, "suffers stress from time to time; the pressure of the sun…" It was silent for a while, then said, "These are the last years of the planet."

We greeted its words with silence, such was the enormity of the concept.

"The last years," I echoed.

"The sun's gravitational force is tearing the planet apart, and has been doing so for millennia; but now has come the time when the integrity of the world will bear no more, and Earth will be torn to pieces. Already the moon has crumbled to dust..."

Cheth said, "To think! The end of the world which has harboured so many great races, so much grand history. The planet has been an arena, upon which has been played out the destiny and fate of countless optimistic races."

It was a humbling thought.

"And this," said Kamis, "is why we were brought here, to the end of time?"

Instead of replying, Rep turned a claw towards the Earth below. The sandstorm had abated, to reveal a flat expanse of shimmering sand. I saw, far below, and made minuscule by our elevation, a procession of… At first I thought them vehicles, but on closer inspection I made out groups of individuals making their way towards the sun at speed.

Cheth banked, and we glided towards the seabed, and the individuals resolved themselves into all manner of strange and wondrous creatures. I beheld a great segmented insect scurrying alongside a creature as golden and proud as a lion, but bi-pedal and clad in robes. I saw something like a jellyfish pulsing along through the air, its polychromatic innards strobing through the spectrum in what might have been some form of arcane language; I saw beings like birds the size of pterosaurs, and rolling balls of sinew that conformed to no life-form I had ever beheld. Among these varied beings I made out familiar figures: crab-beings like Rep running hither and yon as if shepherding the crowds.

Kamis laughed. "But there are hundreds of them! Thousands!"

Across the wide breadth of the seabed, the cavalcade of beings was drawn like iron filings summoned by some invisible magnet towards the beauteous attractor of the dying sun.

"But not all are from Earth?" Cheth said.

"You are correct," Rep said. "Some hail from Mars and the moons of Jupiter, Saturn and Uranus, and beyond. All are races which once dwelled proudly in the solar system."

"And they, too," Kamis asked, "have been accessed, enabled, and brought to fruition?"

Rep waved an acknowledging claw. "That is so."

I said, "So, then, has every sentient being that has ever lived been brought to fruition to witness the end of planet Earth and the solar system?"

There was a pause before Rep said, "Not every being, my friend. Merely… representatives."

We all three allowed this statement to sit in the air, before Cheth said, "But by what right, or by what stroke of fortune, was it deemed that *I* should represent my race?"

This was the question which had sprung to my mind, too.

Rep was silent. At last Kamis prompted, "Well? I think Cheth's query is valid."

"I will explain very soon," was all the crab would say.

I gazed down at the throng, and saw that it was added to all the time by the arrival of more beings from every direction, escorted by their Ky[20] guides.

Then I beheld, among the teeming life down there, something almost human. It was small and ape-like, though walked upright with a noble bearing. I gestured to Rep and said, "A human being, like me?"

Rep responded, "A being which came to sentience on Earth a million years before *Homo sapiens*, but of a different species."

I thought of the scientists working away in the underground bunker, and said, "The scientists we saw – what exactly were they doing?"

Rep tuned an eye-stalk my way. "They were bringing about a rift in space and time."

I gasped, and thought I had an answer. "Our summons here, the scientists... they – you – are sending us back in time to warn our races of the doom that awaits the planet?"

Rep made a sound like laughter. "Such a rationalistic theory, my friend. But what might that achieve? The end of Earth is a fact, an immutable law which cannot be averted. It is, indeed, to be celebrated."

"Ah ha!" said Kamis. "So that is what this great pilgrimage is – a celebration?"

"Not," said Rep, "as such."

"Then what?" asked Cheth.

Instead of replying, Rep spoke hurriedly to Cheth, and in response Cheth dropped so that we were flying low above the seabed, just above the heads – and other appendages – of the marching assembly.

I looked upon the varied life that had shared the solar system, and marvelled.

Ahead, the seabed came to an end, dipped and formed a vast amphitheatre, and gathered within this declivity, washed with the light of the ailing primary, sat, stood, and hovered myriad curious individuals. We came to a halt, hovering above the heads of the crowd, and stared.

And, as we stared, a remarkable thing happened high above the amphitheatre; it was as if the air before the sun had finally succumbed to the great heat and split, for the sky was torn from horizon to zenith to reveal an ellipse of such blinding luminescence that it dazzled the gaze. I turned my head and beheld, to either side of the rent, great silver machines the size of planets with claws which reached out and held open the sides of the blinding ellipse.

Rep gestured. "The last gesture of the Effectuators," it said, "aided by our humble selves."

"But what…?" I managed.

"They were masters of space and time, and we their mere minions, slaves if you like, to do their bidding. But what bidding!"

"Tell us," said Cheth.

"We have helped to open a rift in the fabric of the continuum; we gaze now upon the fundament, the essence that underpins all reality."

"And our presence here?" I asked.

Rep turned to me, and regarded me with its eye-stalks, and paused before saying, "I implied earlier that you represent your race, my friend."

Kamis said, "And we wondered why us, why we of all the millions, the billions, of our race… Why we should be selected for this… honour."

And Rep said, "When I said 'represent your race', that is exactly what I meant." It paused before continuing, "You are not individuals, as such, but distillations of the essences of your respective races."

I felt a welling sadness within me, almost like despair. "But my memories… my loved ones… The love I felt – the love I feel!"

Rep said, "It is valid, my friend, but does not refer to a specific individual. Instead, it is something far greater – the incarnation of the goodness that made your race great."

"And we were brought here for what reason?" asked Kamis. "Surely, not just to witness the end of the Earth?"

Rep waved a claw. "The Effectuators were perhaps the greatest of all the races that ever graced the solar system, and they foresaw an end to all things, not just our sun – but the universe itself."

Something stirred within me at these words, some premonition of what all this was about, and I felt a fluttering sensation within my chest.

"They worked to defy entropy, to abnegate the draconian laws of the universe – the laws which state that all things must end."

"And?" I asked, my voice a tremor.

"And," said Rep, waving towards the rent in space, "they have succeeded. Behold the entrance to another time and space…"

We stared, but comprehension eluded us.

Before we could question Rep further, there was a stirring in the crowd beneath us, a surge forward. I looked ahead and saw that, on the distant horizon, the amphitheatre was emptying of its assembled species, draining like water from a dam.

They were giving themselves to the rent in the space-time continuum.

And we too were moving towards it.

Rep said, "You contain, within you, the essences of your races, the life-force of the universe."

"And you, my friend?" I asked.

"I am a mere guide," Rep said. "I go no further, but will live out my last years among my kind, secure in the knowledge that we have fulfilled the desire of the Effectuators."

"And they?" I Kamis asked.

"They dwell in the universe as beings of energy," Rep said. "Now... go!"

We left Rep, and moved swiftly towards the light, and it was blinding.

And I cried out, reaching for memories. I felt great sadness that *I* was no more than an illusion, and then a welling of rapture that everything I was should amount to such greatness, for I knew then that I – and Kamis and Cheth and the countless others with me – were seeds.

We moved towards the rent, towards the beginning of myriad new universes, and I gave thanks.

And fell into the light.

# The Tragic Affair of the Martian Ambassador

*I wrote the following for an anthology of Sherlock Holmes stories. I've done one other Holmes pastiche before, "the Vanishing of the Atkinsons" for Mike Ashley's New Sherlock Holmes Adventure, which was a straight mainstream detective story. I wanted this tale to be science fiction. It occurred to me that an interesting premise might be the setting of Wells' The War of the Worlds, but with the difference that the Earth was visited by a second, more benign wave of Martians following the viral defeat of the original invaders. Add H.G. Wells and Rebecca West to the mix and you have...*

There commenced in the spring of 1915 one of the most fascinating cases that my friend, Mr Sherlock Holmes, has had the fortune to investigate since the arrival on our planet of the Martians ten years ago.

We were relaxing in our rooms that morning, having recently solved the enigma that came to be known as the Mysterious Affair of the Rosebury Diamonds. I was scanning the Times and my friend, as was his wont of late, was poring over one of a dozen tomes he had purchased from a bookseller on Charing Cross Road.

In 1906, shortly after the establishment of the Martian presence in London and other capitals around the world, my friend took it upon himself to learn the predominant language of the Red Planet. Almost a decade later, thanks to his diligence and exceptional powers of memory, he was practically fluent in that notoriously complex tongue. As a reward he had bought himself a complete set of the *Encyclopaedia Martiannica.*

Now I set aside my paper and glanced across at Holmes. He had taken a break from his studies and was filling his pipe.

"What are you reading about now, Holmes?" I enquired.

He flicked a hand at the open page. "A volume on the biological history of the Martian race," said he. "Fascinating. Did you know,

Watson, that the gestation cycle of a pregnant Martian female is a little over three Terran years?"

"I must admit my ignorance in that area," said I.

"And were you aware, moreover… Hullo, and what's this?" he said, glancing across at the window.

The spring sunlight had been occluded suddenly, as if by a storm cloud, and as we strode across the room and stared out we beheld the reason. A Martian tripod, fully a hundred feet high, stood in the street outside.

"Curiouser and curiouser," Holmes commented, for a platform was descending from the underbelly of the cowled vehicle and riding upon it was a Martian.

Now, for all that the Martians occupy our planet in their hundreds of thousands, it is not an everyday occurrence that one of their number is seen, as it were, in the flesh. Their singular three-legged transportation devices might ubiquitously prowl the capital from Richmond to East Ham, and from Barnet to Croydon, but the creatures themselves show a distinct inclination towards privacy.

Not, however, this individual – for it stepped from the platform and trundled on its many puckered tentacles across the road and on to the pavement.

Holmes rubbed his hands together in delight. "Why, I do believe, Watson, that the Martian is making a bee-line towards 221b!"

Indeed the alien was hauling itself up the steps towards our front door. We repaired to our respective chairs and made ourselves ready for the audience. I was, I have no hesitation in admitting, more than a little excited at the prospect.

A minute later Mrs Hudson, appearing unaccustomedly flustered, burst into the room. "Oh, Mr Holmes!" she cried. "Would you credit it, but there's one of those 'orrible Martian creatures downstairs, and it said it wants to see you promptly!"

My friend smiled. "Then if you would kindly show the fellow up, Mrs Hudson."

"And leave its dreadful slime all over my new carpets?"

"I will personally pay for their cleaning. Now, I rather think that time is of the essence."

With an indrawn breath, Mrs Hudson departed.

Evidently our extra-planetary visitor, for all its many tentacles – or perhaps because of them – found the ascent of the staircase something of a trial, for it was a good five minutes before Mrs Hudson flung open the door and stood aside as the Martian shuffled into the room.

We rose to our feet, as the occasion seemed to demand, and I stared in fascination at our visitor.

We are all aware, from the many illustrations provided by our national dailies, of the appearance of the beings from the Red Planet. Now, however prepared I might have been, the sight of the creature in such close proximity provoked in me the contradictory emotions of fascination and repulsion, for the Martian was truly hideous.

It stood perhaps five feet tall, its shorter lower half consisting of six writhing tentacles most easily described as octopoid. Its larger upper section, or torso, however, bore no relation to that of any terrestrial creature, and this perhaps accounted for my horror.

Set into the oily brown skin of its torso was a quivering, v-shaped mouth and two vast, cloudy eyes. Strapped around its mid-section was a belt, fastened to which was a small black box.

However uncomely its appearance, that was nothing beside the revulsion I experienced as the creature's peculiar body odour wafted my way – a scent that combined the stench of putrid carrion with the sweet reek of rotting fruit.

Holmes, maintaining an enviable *savoir fare* in the face of the noisome aroma, gestured the alien to a *chaise longue*, the only piece of furniture in the room able to contain its broad bulk.

The Martian sat down, arranging its several limbs across the brocade in a manner at once businesslike yet prim. As we watched, the peculiar v-shaped mouth quivered and a series of rapid burbles, and not a few belches, filled the air.

"Mr Holmes, Mr Watson –" the tinny translation issued from a grille in the black box seconds later, "I am Gruvlax-Xenxa-Schmee, deputy ambassador to the British Empire, and I have come today to request your investigational services."

Holmes leaned forward, evidently excited, and it was a temptation beyond his powers of resistance to reply to the deputy-ambassador in its own tongue. My friend gave vent to a horrible series of eructations which surely taxed the elasticity of his larynx.

The Martian flung several of its tentacles into the air and replied excitedly, "But you have mastered our language as no other Earthling yet, Mr Holmes!"

My friend laughed. "We should proceed, for the sake of my friend Mr Watson, in English." He turned to me and said, "I asked, Watson, as to the nature of the investigation."

Presently the creature replied, "I am afraid that that should remain undisclosed until you have agreed to accompany me to the ambassador's residence, where I will furnish you with all the relevant details."

Holmes harrumphed, not taken by such a stipulation. His curiosity, however, was piqued. He said to me, "This can be no little mater, Watson, if the ambassador himself requires our presence." To the Martian he said, "Very well, Mr Gruvlax-Xenxa-Schmee. Shall we hasten to the embassy?"

"We will avail ourselves of my tripod," said the Martian.

Holmes jumped to his feet. "The game's afoot Watson," said he, and reached for his cape.

To stride the boroughs of London as if on the shoulders of a giant!

We sat ensconced in comfortable armchairs in the hooded cockpit of the tripod and goggled in amazement at the business of London passing to and fro far below. Tiny cars powered by the latest Martian technology beetled along like trilobites, and in the air the first of the flying machines, owned by intrepid – and wealthy – Earthmen buzzed about like insects.

The ride was over all too soon. What seemed like minutes later we were deposited outside the Martian embassy in Grosvenor Square and ushered up the steps by the deputy ambassador. In due course we entered the sitting room of the penthouse suite and paused beside a polished timber door.

Without further ado Gruvlax-Xenxa-Schmee said, "I made the discovery this morning, Mr Holmes. Beyond the door is the ambassador's bedroom, and it is my habit to enter at eight, once the ambassador has risen, to apprise him of the day's agenda."

Holmes fixed the deputy with an eagle eye. "And this morning?"

Gruvlax-Xenxa-Schmee reached a tentacle towards the door and turned the handle. The door swung open, and the Martian stood aside and gestured for us to enter.

Holmes stepped forth with alacrity, and a little more hesitantly I followed.

We were in a bed-chamber dominated by a large double bed, upon which reposed the bulk of the Martian ambassador.

I did not require a doctorate in Martian medicine to ascertain that the ambassador was quite dead.

"Stabbed," Holmes opined, "by a sharp implement in the centre of its torso – the area in the Martian body where the major pulmonary organ is located."

Gruvlax-Xenxa-Schmee shuffled back and forth beside the bed, obviously in a state of great agitation or grief. "We have summoned our finest investigational team from Mars," it said, "but it will be several weeks before they arrive on Earth. Also upon that ship is the ambassador's life-mate, come to retrieve her partner's corpse for burial in the sands of our home planet."

I stood over the bed and gazed down at the dead Martian. Added to its usual odour was the obnoxious stench of escaped bodily fluids. I withdrew a handkerchief and covered my mouth and nose.

Ichor, sulphurous yellow and viscid, had leaked from the wound in its torso and pooled in the sheets around its bulk. The vast eyes were open, and stared blindly at the ceiling. Its v-shaped mouth likewise gaped, as if in the emitting of a final painful cry.

Beside the bed was a small table upon which lay several envelopes, each one slit neatly open.

"And you say the door was locked?" asked Holmes.

The Martian replied, "From the inside, by the ambassador."

"Was he is the habit of locking his bedroom door?"

"The ambassador valued his privacy."

"I see," said Holmes. "I take it you had a spare key?"

"That is so. And I fetched it when the ambassador failed to respond to my summons at eight."

"And the key, Deputy Ambassador – is it kept in a place from where others might easily take it?"

"It is kept in an unlocked drawer in the bureau," it replied, gesturing to the adjacent sitting room with a quivering tentacle.

"How many members of staff would have access to the key?"

"Just four: two of my own people, and the two humans who work in the embassy."

"If you would kindly summon them forthwith for questioning, I would be most grateful."

The Martian shuffled from the room. Seconds later Holmes declared, "Hullo, what's this?"

In three strides he had crossed to the window, which stood open six inches. He lifted it further and peered out. I joined him; the drop to the gravelled forecourt below was in excess of forty feet, and no convenient drainpipe, wisteria or the like, clad the wall to provide suitable access.

Holmes stood back and contemplated the wall below the window-sill.

I saw what attracted his attention – a gouge in the wallpaper four inches beneath the sill, and an abrasion on the paint of the woodwork itself.

"But what could it be?" I asked.

"If the ambassador was in the habit of keeping his window open at night, and an intruder armed with a grapple and rope… You catch my line of reasoning, Watson? Then again, there might be an entirely innocent explanation for the marks."

I examined the wall more closely, and when I turned from the window Holmes was tucking something into his breast pocket, which he had presumably taken from the bedside table. There was an expression on his face which I have beheld many times before: the aquiline glint in his eye that betokened the fact that he had garnered what he considered to be a significant clue.

Before I could question him, however, the deputy ambassador returned.

"The staff are gathered and await you next door, Mr Holmes," it said.

"And you have been in the employ of the embassy for how long?" Holmes asked.

"Three years this May," replied the gentleman by the name of Herbert, a sallow man in his late forties with expressive, melancholy eyes and a straggling moustache. In a singular recapitulation of the physiology of his employers, Herbert had short legs and a stocky, barrel-like torso.

"And your position in the embassy?"

"I work as a… you might call it a scientific advisor to the ambassador and his staff. I liaise between the Martian scientists and engineers who visit our world with their wonders, and their opposite numbers on Earth." He spoke in an odd, high-pitched voice, with not a little trace of cockney in the vowels.

"And you trained at…?"

"The Royal College of Science, under none other than the great Professor Huxley himself."

Holmes smiled. "For a man of humble origins, Herbert, you have acquitted yourself remarkably well."

"Not too badly, if I say so myself – for the son of a draper," Herbert said.

My friend cleared his throat. "Now, to the matter at hand. In your time working in the embassy have you had reason to notice any enmity being directed towards the ambassador?"

Herbert shook his head. "None whatsoever, sir. The ambassador is… was… well liked, by both Martians and humans. He was a wise and generous employer. I cannot imagine who might have done this."

"Are you aware of the political factions that exist among the Martians? We well know that there was political strife, not to say animosity, between certain nations before their arrival here."

The scientific liaison officer shook his head. "I know of certain political differences between the Martians, yes, but I was not aware that such differences existed between the ambassador and his staff, or any other Martians who had dealings with him on Earth."

"Very well. Now… we come to the business of what happened last night. Gruvlax-Xenxa-Schmee last saw the ambassador at eleven o'clock, at which time the ambassador repaired to his bed-chamber and locked the door. It is my estimation that the ambassador died at some time between eleven and six or seven this morning… though I admit I am not an expert on matters of Martian pathology. Now, where were you between these hours?"

"I have a room in the basement of the embassy, sir. I retired at nine, where I wrote for two hours before going to bed."

"You keep a diary?"

Herbert smiled. "I write fiction," he said. "Though nothing of what I write finds favour with publishers' current tastes. Too fantastical," he finished.

Holmes murmured his condolences. "Perhaps what is needed in these fantastic times is a little more social realism," said he, before returning to the matter at hand. "And you rose at…?"

"Eight, as usual. It was then that Gruvlax-Xenxa-Schmee summoned me with the alarming news."

Holmes nodded sagely, regarding his long fingers splayed on the table-top before him. He then looked up at Herbert. "And I take it that you know where the spare key to the ambassador's bed-chamber is kept?"

"Yes, sir. In the bureau in this very room."

"To which you have access?"

Herbert nodded. "Yes, sir."

"That will be all, Mr Wells. Will you be kind enough to send in Miss West?"

Herbert opened the communicating door to be met in the threshold by a vision of striking loveliness, a woman I guessed to be in her mid-twenties, raven-haired, pale skinned and serious. I noted that I was not alone in observing what passed between them: Holmes watched the couple as they gripped each other's hands and uttered what might have been reassuring words, before Miss West smiled bravely and strode with exceptional deportment into the room.

She seated herself at the table. "Mr Holmes, Mr Watson; it is an honour indeed to meet at last such illustrious upholders of the judiciary. I have followed your exploits with considerable interest, gentlemen."

Holmes smiled thinly. "In which case you will have no objections to aiding our enquiries?"

The slightest frowned marred, for a second, the perfection of her alabaster forehead. "Of course not, Mr Holmes."

The interview that followed was the swiftest I have ever seen my friend conduct. It seemed barely two minutes from when Miss West entered the room to the time she swept out.

"If you could inform me of the position you hold in the embassy, Miss West, and the duration you have been here?"

She regarded Holmes with a level gaze, her vast brown eyes

unwavering. "I am… was… employed as the private secretary to Yerkell-Jheer-Carral, the late Martian ambassador, and I have held the position for a little over six months."

"And your duties entailed?"

Was it my imagination, or did I see a flare of anger in those serene chestnut eyes? "What do you expect the duties of a private secretary to be, Mr Holmes? I arranged the ambassador's itinerary, dealt with his correspondence, interviews and the like."

"Would you say that, over the months you have held the post, you have come to know the ambassador?"

She frowned as she contemplated the question. "I am not sure that one is able to come to *know*, with any certitude, the person of an extra-planetary being."

"But did he seem, in your dealings with him, a fair employer?"

She shrugged expressively. "I had no… complaints."

"And between the hours of eleven last night and seven this morning, you were on the premises of the embassy?"

"I have an apartment nearby, but last night I was working late. It was after midnight when I left my office and made my way home."

"And when was the last time you set eyes on Mr Yerkell-Jheer-Carral?"

"That would be around seven, when I finished taking that day's dictation."

My friend then surprised me by saying, "Thank you, Miss West. That will be all, for now."

Miss West inclined her fine head towards Holmes and myself, then rose and hurried from the table.

She was almost at the door when Holmes asked, "One more question, if I might, Miss West?"

She turned. "Yes?"

"How long have you known the ambassador's scientific liaison officer, Mr Wells?"

"For a little short for six months," she replied.

"And how would you describe your relationship with him?"

Something very much like annoyance, or perhaps indignation, flared in her gaze. She said defiantly, "Mr Wells and I are engaged to be married, Mr Holmes," whereupon she turned and swept from the room.

For the next hour we interviewed the two Martian staff members, attachés who liaised on matters of state with the British government. They could tell us little about the ambassador, other than that they held him in high regard, were terribly shocked by his passing, and had little to vouchsafe on the matter of the political factions that had riven the Martian nations preceding their arrival on Earth. When asked if the ambassador had enemies among the many Martians in London, each responded with surprised sounds which their box-translators struggled to interpret.

In due course he dismissed the second attaché and turned to Gruvlax-Xenxa-Schmee. "You might inform Scotland Yard of what has happened. And I suggest that you authorise your medical authorities to deal with the ambassador's corpse."

Gruvlax-Xenxa-Schmee waved a tentacle. "Inspector Lestrade is on his way as we speak," it said, "and the body will be removed just as soon as he has conducted his enquiries."

"And I wonder what good old Lestrade will make of the sad affair?" Holmes said in an aside to me. "Come, Watson, we have learned as much as is to be learned here. We continue the investigation elsewhere."

"And where might that be?" I asked as we took our leave of the embassy.

Holmes smiled thinly. "We are heading for Madame Rochelle's," he said.

I echoed the name. "But isn't that…?" I began.

"Indeed it is, Watson. Madame Rochelle's is perhaps the most exclusive brothel in London."

"I'm not at all sure…" I began as we paced down a narrow alleyway off the Strand, glancing over my shoulder to ensure that we were not being observed.

"Curb your fears, Watson. We have penetrated more insalubrious premises in the course of our investigations. Aha… this must be it."

A dark recess gave access to a door, upon which Holmes rapped with his cane. A second later the door opened and a thin face peered out.

My friend whipped a card from his pocket, showed it to the

doorman, and stepped inside.

"Where on Earth did you come by the card?" I whispered as I followed Holmes down a darkened corridor.

"Where else, Watson, but in the ambassador's bed-chamber."

"Ah! So that's why you were looking like the cat with the cream," I said.

Holmes paused and turned to me. "Your powers of observation, Watson, are as acute as ever."

I huffed at this, then said, "And what else did you find in the bed-chamber?"

My friend gave a short laugh. "I found nothing, Watson. That is, I did not find what I was looking for."

"And what might that have been?"

"The opener with which the ambassador had slit his letters."

"The murder weapon!" I expostulated.

"A brilliant deduction, my friend. Now, I think through here…"

He opened a green baize door and instantly we were assailed by loud music – Debussy, I thought – from one of the new-fangled Martian harmony-grams, along with the overwhelming reek of perfume and a sight to shock the most jaded of sensibilities.

Young ladies, in various stages of *déshabillé*, disported themselves around the room upon chesterfields and divans, courted – shall we say? – by their suitors. It was only then that the need for the perfume became apparent: several among the clients were none other than malodorous Martians, and it was an odd, not to say nauseating, sight indeed to see the ivory limbs of the young ladies entwined with the writhing tentacles of their otherworldly patrons.

"I never even dreamed…" I began.

Holmes commented, "Some Martians find our women irresistible, Watson."

"What shocks me is that some of our women succumb to their advances."

"Such is the tragedy of their circumstances," said Holmes with a lugubrious expression.

A scantily-clad woman of middle years advanced upon us, smiling. "Welcome, gentlemen. If I might take your coats…"

Homes proffered his calling card and said, "If you would be kind enough to present this to Madam Rochelle, and impress upon her that we need speak to her about a matter of the utmost importance."

Two minutes later we were ushered into a highly-scented and sweltering boudoir. A buxom woman, whose wrinkled flesh spoke of advanced years, sat upon what appeared to be a throne beside a blazing fire.

"Mr Holmes hisself!" she declared in a Hackney shriek. "Never thought I'd see the great detective on my turf, so to speak. Are you sure I can't tempt you with one of my more beautiful girls?"

Holmes maintained an admirable élan. "We are here to investigate a murder, madam."

"A murder? Who's been murdered? I assure you none of my girls –"

"I understand that none other than the Martian ambassador himself, a certain Yerkell-Jheer-Carral, was a frequent visitor to your establishment?"

"'Was' is right, Mr Holmes. The ambassador stopped coming here about six months ago, and I right miss him I do. The ambassador was a bit of a character, you see."

My friend considered her words and stroked his chin with a long forefinger. "That is interesting, and informative," he murmured to himself. "Now, could you tell me if any of your ladies in the habit of visiting the ambassador at the Martian embassy?"

"What? And you think I send my girls out into the city? I protect my girls, I do."

"I am sure you do, Madam Rochelle," said Holmes. "I wonder if you can recall, when the ambassador visited your establishment, if he exhibited a preference for a certain type of lady?"

Madam Rochelle thought about that. "He liked 'em dark, Mr Holmes. No blondes for the ambassador. Dark and sultry was how he liked his wimmen."

In due course Homes thanked Madam Rochelle, assured her once again that we did not care to avail ourselves of the pleasures of her establishment, and withdrew.

We escaped the cloying confines of Madam Rochelle's and once again breathed the refreshing spring air of the Strand. Holmes made a bee-line for a Communications Kiosk – yet another wonder for which we had to thank the Martians – on the corner of the Strand and Northumberland Avenue. "Excuse me one moment, Watson," he said, and squeezed his angular frame into the kiosk.

He emerged minutes later and explained, "I contacted Mr Wells and Miss West, and arranged to meet them, in secrecy, on Hampstead Heath at six." Without further ado he crossed the pavement and slipped into W.H. Smith's, emerging a minute later to hail a passing taxi.

"And now?" I asked as we climbed aboard.

"To the Martian embassy," Holmes said, and seconds later we were hurtling through the streets of the capital.

An underling Martian showed us into the embassy and summoned the deputy-ambassador.

Holmes asked if he might again examine the ambassador's bed-chamber, and Gruvlax-Xenxa-Schmee escorted us up the stairs to the penthouse suite.

Holmes hurried over to the bed while I remained on the threshold with the deputy, stopped in my tracks by the foul stench issuing from the corpse. Holmes for his part seemed not to notice the aroma. With his back to me he appeared to be searching through the late ambassador's inert tentacles.

"Aha!" he said at last, and turned on me a look of triumph.

Gruvlax-Xenxa-Schmee perambulated itself past me and into the room. It gave vent to a series of oesophageal belches which the box at its midriff translated as, "Mr Holmes, if I might enquire as to how the investigation proceeds?"

"I am happy to inform you that the case is solved," Holmes said. He stood beside the bed and gestured at the tangle of dead limbs sprawling across the counterpane. "My initial examination of the corpse failed to locate the implement which caused the fatal injury for the very good reason that it was concealed beneath the ambassador's forelimb."

Gruvlax-Xenxa-Schmee hurried to the bed and I, gagging at the stench, joined them.

I stared down at the tangle of tentacles and beheld, gripped in a suckered pseudopod, a blood-stained letter-knife.

The Martian spoke. "Are you saying, Mr Holmes, that…?" it began.

My friend said, "My investigations led me, in due course, to an establishment at which the pleasures of the flesh might be indulged by those of little self-restraint. It is my painful duty to inform you that the ambassador was a frequent visitor to this establishment, where he developed a predilection for human ladies of a certain type."

Before me, Gruvlax-Xenxa-Schmee appeared to slump. "I was aware of his weakness," it said, "and more than once attempted to reason with his Excellency, to no avail."

"It is my opinion," said Holmes, "that remorse overcame the ambassador, and in the throes of self-recrimination, and guilt at his unfaithfulness to his mate – at this very moment travelling the gulf between Mars and Earth – he took his own life."

The deputy-ambassador said, "A tragic affair, Mr Holmes…"

In due course we took our leave, and, as we hurried across the square towards the taxi rank, I said doubtfully, "Suicide? But… how was it that you didn't find the letter-knife when you first examined the corpse?"

"All will be revealed in time, Watson. Have patience." He opened the rear door of the taxi and slipped inside. "To Hampstead Heath," he told the driver.

We came to the crest of the hill and stood in silence, all London spread before us. The sun was setting, and a roseate light bathed the capital. I made out familiar landmarks, St Pauls and Trafalgar column, and more recent additions to the city's skyline: the spaceyard in Streatham constructed by the Martians, and the stanchioned air-port for the new flying machines over at Bermondsey. Prominent across the city were the towering tripods, stilled now after the activity of the day, hooded and slightly sinister. Soon, when the sun went down, they would begin their curiously mournful and eerie ululations, the meaning of which was still a mystery to us humans.

"Who would have guessed, Watson, that in the last years of the nineteenth century, our world was being watched keenly and closely by intelligences greater than, and yet as mortal as, our own?" Holmes sighed. "Who would have guessed that, in time, they would cross the vast gulfs of space and settle our planet? If that first invasion had succeeded, if the microbes of this world had not fought off the invaders as successfully as any army, then life on Earth would now be under the yoke of terrible oppressors. Give thanks that a second, more altruistic Martian nation followed, who worked to cure the microbial disease that did for their cousins, and who brought a new, technological age to our planet. And yet, Watson…"

"And yet?"

"And yet, the Martians are an invading army still, for all their technological accomplishment and largesse, and they bring with them their own ignorance, and evil."

He paused, his aquiline face plunged in melancholy introspection for a space, and then he roused himself and pointed. "Look, Watson, down by that oak. Mr Wells and Miss West, holding hands like the lovers they are. Shall we join them?"

We made our way down the incline and met the pair beneath the spreading boughs. Both looked suspicious, West's beautiful visage drawn and even paler than usual.

Wells stepped forward. "You said you had news…?" he began.

"The case is resolved," said Holmes. "We located the weapon."

At this Wells flinched. "Located…?" he echoed.

"It was concealed beneath the ambassadors tangled limbs," Holmes explained.

Miss West stared at him. "But isn't it curious that you did not find the knife when you first examined the corpse?"

"Not in the slightest," replied Holmes, "for the knife was not in situ when I first made my examination."

"What?" I cried.

"Then how…?" Wells began.

"I placed it there just one hour ago, when I entered the ambassador's bed-chamber for the last time."

I stared aghast at my friend. "Do you know what you're saying, Holmes?" I expostulated. "Why… but that means the ambassador cannot have taken his own life!"

Holmes smiled, and turned to Mr Wells and Miss West. "That is correct, is it not? Would you care to explain?"

Miss West opened her mouth, quite shocked. "Why, I have no idea what you mean…"

"Come, my dear. I am quite aware of the ambassador's… predilections, shall we say?"

At this, Miss West broke down and sobbed. Wells embraced her, and it was a minute before she regained her composure, looked Holmes squarely in the eye, and said, "Six months ago, upon my appointment as the ambassador's private secretary, he made his feelings known. I was revolted, of course, though I was well aware of the… the tastes of some of his kind. The ambassador, for all his status, was not exempt from these depravities… and with increasing insistence he proceeded to press himself upon me. Last night he asked me into his room, ostensibly to dictate a last letter. However…" She sobbed, biting her knuckle. "Oh, it was horrible, horrible! His strength, his ghastly, overwhelming…"

Holmes reached out and touched her shoulder. "Please, there is no need to go on."

Wells interposed. In a trembling voice he took up the story. "I was passing the room, Holmes, when I heard Rebecca's cries. I fetched the key and let myself into the bed-chamber, and what I saw there…" He shook his head bitterly, his expression wretched. "I was beside myself with rage, sir, and blinded to the consequences took up the letter-knife and… and plunged it into the horror's torso…" He looked up, defiantly. "I am not proud of what I did, but my love for Rebecca and my revulsion at the ambassador's vile actions…" He paused, then went on. "I opened the window and gouged a mark in the wall beneath, to make it appear that the murder was the work of an intruder. I then left the embassy and disposed of the knife in the Thames."

He looked up, staring Holmes in the eye, and said, "I do not regret what I did, for the animal had it coming to him, and like a man I will face the consequences. If you inform Scotland Yard of my actions, I will have my day in court."

Homes smiled at this, then said, "Well said, but it will take more than pretty rhetoric to persuade me that what you said is the truth of it."

I stared at my friend. "What the deuce are you driving at, Holmes?"

The great detective turned to Miss West, and said, "Well?"

Miss West faced the detective foursquare, thought for a space, and began, "I –"

Wells gripped her hand. "Rebecca…"

"No, Bertie," said she, "the truth is better out… You are correct, Mr Holmes, Bertie did not kill the ambassador in a fit of rage." She took a deep breath, then said, "*I* did… for when he pressed himself upon me, held me down with his tentacles and… and proceeded to… You must understand that I was beside myself with terror, and when I saw the letter-knife on the bedside table, I reached out and grasped it and…" She stopped, almost out of breath. "I did what I did, Mr Holmes, in self-defence, but I too will face the consequences if that is what you feel right and proper."

Holmes shook his head. "As far as the authorities are concerned, both human and Martian, the affair is closed. The ambassador killed himself in a fit of remorse and guilt for his philandering with human women. The Martian judiciary will not arrive for another five weeks, by which time what evidence there is will be corrupted. While not condoning your actions, I understand the terrible fear that drove you to commit the deed."

"You mean…?"

"In my opinion you have suffered enough, Miss West. Naught will be gained by hauling you before the court, for while a human law might have sympathy with your plight, I cannot say the same for the Martian judiciary."

She stared at him open-mouthed, tears glistening in her eyes.

"If I were you," Holmes went on, "I would leave the embassy, turn your back on the terrible memories of last night and start anew. Your secret is safe with Watson and me."

Wells said, "Why, but I cannot thank you enough, Mr Holmes!"

Miss West stepped forward and placed a kiss on the detective's cheek. "Thank you," she murmured.

Presently we watched them step from beneath the boughs of the oak and, hand in hand, walk into the diminishing twilight of the heath.

In due course we made our way back to Baker Street. Holmes lit his pipe and pulled upon it ruminatively. I stared up at the stars scattered brightly across the heavens and said, "You think they'll be all right, Holmes?"

"They have talent, Watson. I've read a little of Miss West's journalism, and very impressed I was. And maybe Wells's jottings will come to something."

For a space I was lost in a brown study as I pondered the coming of the Martians and the many wondrous, and not so wondrous, incidents their arrival had entailed.

We strode on in companionable silence as the darkness deepened around us, and at last, from all across London, near and far, there sounded the first of the tripods' strange and mournful cries.

"Ulla, ulla," they called dolorously into the warm night air. "Ulla, ulla..."

# Bukowski on Mars, with Beer

*I've been reading Charles Bukowski, on and off, for more than thirty years – I find his pared down, grim, often shocking stories and novels compulsive. I'm also often appalled by his attitude towards his fellow man, women, life... But I keep reading because I find his honesty refreshing and unique. There are no other writers I can think of who present their lives with such unremitting candour. He lived a hard life – until his late success – and that's what he wrote about, warts and all. I've often wondered what he would have made of the future – and then it came to me to resurrect him on Mars and find out.*

"Wake up, Buk!"

I opened my eyes. A guy a silver suit was standing by the bed.

I said, "Hey, man, it ain't Buk as in fuck. It's Buk as in puke, okay?"

The man smiled and it reminded me of my father.

I sat up. "Where am I?"

That last I remembered I was in a bar someplace in downtown LA. I recalled being thrown into the street and passing out. I felt fine now, not even a hangover.

"Where's Jane?"

"Buk," he said, getting it right this time. "Lie down. Listen to me. You're a long way from home."

"I am, huh? Get me a beer, okay?"

He reached out behind me and came back with a bottle of beer. I didn't recognize the brand but I wasn't complaining. I chugged it down. It was good and cold and I felt better.

I looked around. I was in a circular room with a good view over red sand.

"Listen, buddy, why not tell me what the fuck's going on?"

The man looked at me. "You're on Mars, Buk," he said.

"You're taking it well."

I took it well when my father strapped me every day for years, I took it well when big fuckers tried to beat me up in bars in LA and New Orleans and Atlanta and Pittsburgh and New York. The trick was not to show what you're feeling inside. The trick was to freeze.

The guy in the silver suit said I was on Mars and I froze.

"So tell me," I said, "just how come I ended up on Mars? And get me another beer."

He got it.

I chugged it down.

He said, "We brought you back to life."

"I was dead?"

"Yes."

"And you brought me back? So you can bring Jane back, too?"

"No, Buk. No, I'm sorry."

I took another swallow of beer.

"So why me?"

"Because you're one of the greats, Buk. We've brought back the greats."

He watched me. I said nothing.

Hear that, you fuckers? Hear that, Pa, all you bastards who said I was shit, hear that, all you phonies in all the cities who took one look and said no?

"One of the greats?" I said. "When did I die?"

"March, 1994."

"Jee-sus fucking Christ..."

The guy gave me a funny look. "You don't remember?"

I shook my head. "Last I recall, it's... '73."

"You lived another twenty years, Buk. You became famous. Your books sold millions, you were big in France, Germany."

"So why can't I remember any of that?"

"It sometimes happens. Retrieval can result in memory loss, often only short term. Your memories will return."

I saluted him with the bottle. I had that to look forward to: remembering my successful future.

I laughed. One of the greats?

And I was on Mars.

I swung myself off the bed. "I need to take a dump. Where's the john?"

He was still there when I got back. "Who else?"

"Excuse me?"

"Who else you brought back? The greats."

"Artists. Composers. Other writers."

"Writers like who? Celine?"

He shook his head. "No, not Celine."

"Hamsun?"

"Knut Hamsun? Yes, all the Nobel prize winners."

"How'd he take it, being brought back?"

The guy nodded. "He's fine. He's writing. He has a little place on the slopes of Olympus Mons."

"Lawrence?"

"D.H. or T.E?"

"D.H.."

"Yes. He took it badly at first, but he adjusted. He's traveling – crossing the Mare Acidalium, the last we heard."

"And Doe– Doe–"

"Dostoevsky?"

"That's the guy."

"We made the retrieval, but..." The guy shrugged.

"What happened?"

"He went mad. It sometimes – very infrequently – happens."

"Mailer?"

"Yes. He's fine. Doing the celebrity circuit."

I thought some. "How about Hemingway?"

"Yes. He's living nearby, as are most of the other retrievals. You'll meet them all, eventually."

"Fuck that. I didn't want to meet other writers when I was alive, and I sure don't want to meet the fuckers now."

"That's fine, but I think you'll change your mind, in time. It's somewhat therapeutic, let's say, to meet others of your kind."

I took a long swallow of cold beer.

"But you didn't bring Jane back?"

"I'm sorry."

"But you could? I mean, you have the ability to do it, yeah?"

He would not meet my gaze. "We only brought back the greats–"

"Listen, buddy, Jane was great."

"I'm sure she was, Buk, but–"

Something tore open inside me, something big and cold and gray.

He said, "You must be hungry. I'll get you some food. Then you can rest a while, sleep. In the morning I'll show you around. Now, food. What would you like?"

I was hungry. "Hamburger and fries. You got those? And some wine? You have wine on Mars?"

"We have the finest vineyards in the solar system growing on the slopes of Elysium Mons"

"Riesling, sweet and cold?"

"I'll see what I can do."

The guy left the room through a sliding door.

I drank my beer.

In the morning I woke up and went to the john and puked and I felt better after that. I got a beer from the cold chest behind the bed and chugged it down, and then the guy in the silver suit came and said he'd show me around. I said okay, but would there be beer? He said there'd be plenty of beer.

We left the room and walked into warm sunlight, down a path in a concrete complex with silver domes in the red sand. I was wearing old chinos and an old shirt, just like old times.

The guy didn't offer his name and I didn't ask.

We came to an open buggy with big wheels like beach balls and the guy said climb in. I got in the passenger seat and the guy indicated the back seat, a cooler there. I got myself a beer and drank and we set off.

We drove out of the complex of domes and into the red desert. The guy told me a whole bunch of stuff about the terraforming of Mars. Most of it I didn't understand, and I wasn't interested enough to ask. The bottom line was that mankind had spread from Earth and was living on Mars and some of the moons of Saturn and Jupiter, spread like a disease.

Once when I turned in the seat to get anther beer, I looked back at the complex we'd left. The domes glittered in the morning sunlight.

After an hour we arrived at another complex in the desert, and this one had factories with great pipes coming from them and spreading out across the desert.

"These are the lungs of the planet," the guy said. He told me that a whole load of stuff was pumped into the Martian atmosphere to keep in breathable. I didn't see a single person anywhere about the place.

We passed the lungs of the planet and moved further into the desert, and I sat in the passenger seat and drank beer after beer.

The guy said, "I make a point of reading all the work of the retrievals I'll be working with."

"That so?"

"I've read practically everything you've ever written."

I was impressed. There was a lot of it. "So what you make of it? My guess, a guy like you..." I gestured with the bottle. "Probably means jack shit to you."

He said, "Buk, I was appalled, but fascinated at the same time, I must admit."

I saluted him with my bottle.

"The drinking, the women... that was incomprehensible enough, but what really appalled me was your apathy."

I shrugged. I couldn't be bothered to argue. The only time I ever defended myself was in a fist-fight. "So why the fuck did you read the stuff?"

"Because I was paid to do so, Buk."

"Pretty easy job, as I see it, sitting on your crack reading a whole bunch of stuff. Even stuff you didn't like."

He ignored that. "Your apathy really astonished me, Buk. You were interested in nothing but drinking and copulating and the races..."

"And boxing and books," I reminded him. "I read some, too."

"And even here, now, Buk – you're just not one bit interested in the wonders of the modern age, are you?

He gestured at something sailing by in the sky. It looked light and airy, like a kite made from aluminum and tinfoil, only it was about the size of an aircraft hangar.

I remembered the skyscrapers and the railroads, the Golden Gate Bridge and the Saturn V rocket. I said, "Show me wonders of the modern age and all I see are rich fuckers getting richer."

"You don't see progress?"

"Progress is just another word for shitting on those at the bottom."

He said, "You're ignorant."

I stared at him. "Everyone is ignorant."

We drove on some. He said, "Why did you write?"

I thought about that. "Because I had to."

"Why did you write the kind of stuff that you wrote?"

I thought some more. "Because I lived the kind of life I lived."

"A life of ignorance and apathy and quiet desperation."

I didn't argue. I looked down at my body. It was the body of a seventy-three year old, but the strange thing was I felt young and strong.

I said, "Pull up."

He looked at me. "What?"

"Stop."

"We're in the middle of the desert. Why–?"

"Stop the fucking car and we'll get out and fight."

I wanted to feel what it was like to fight again, knuckle on bone, I wanted to feel his fist on my jaw. And I wanted to wipe the smug smile from the fucker's face.

"I'm not stopping, Buk."

"Then shut the fuck up," I said.

We came to a sprawling settlement in the desert. We traveled through it on an elevated road. I made out what looked like factories, and then some domes. The thing was, these domes were situated in the middle of big green lawns.

I laughed.

The guy said, "What's so funny."

I said, "You even brought lawns from Earth!"

He said, "You don't like lawns, do you, Buk."

"Lawns make me want to puke."

We drove on. I said, "Slow down."

I saw a broad in a bikini sun-bathing on one of the lawns down there. She stood up as we passed, took off her sun-glasses and watched us: tall and tanned, with a nice ass and stacked.

"Whoa!" I yelled and waved my bottle at her.

We shot past, back into the desert. The guy was gripping the steering wheel, staring ahead. He was saying, "We don't have cities, as such, but small settlements scattered across the face of the planet, manufactories run by a skeleton staff employing AIs..." Blah, blah, fucking blah.

I tuned him out and got another beer. I was getting drunk and the sun was getting hot out there in the desert.

I said, "So why did you bring us back? The Greats?"

He said, "So you can write, and compose, and paint."

"You got no writers and composers and painters on Mars?"

"We have artists of all kinds, yes. But we wanted to resurrect the greats of Earth."

I swallowed some beer and looked ahead. Heat shimmered in the distance above the red sands. I said, "So you want me to write?"

"We'd like that, yes."

"Write what?"

"Whatever you like. Write about your life on Earth." He looked at me. "We'll get you a dome, a word processor."

"A what?"

He thought about it and said, "A computer, so you can write."

"Fuck a computer, buddy. I want a typer. A Remington upright, okay?"

"That might be difficult..." he started.

I said, "You bring the greats back to life from bone and shit, and you can't get me a Remington typer?"

"I'll see what we can do."

We arrived back at the complex and the guy said, "Would you like to go to a bar?"

I stared at him. Was he joking? "That's the first sensible thing you said all day."

We parked and climbed out and walked along a concourse between silver domes to a patio area around a pool. A crowd of men and women sat around the pool drinking. The guys looked like a bunch of phonies but most of the women were lookers.

We went into a dome set out with tables and chairs, clean and dead. Not my kind of place at all. We sat at a table overlooking the pool and the guy said, "Beer?"

"Make it Jack Daniels. A bottle."

He came back with a quart and I sat and drank and watched the beautiful people talk and laugh and jump into the pool.

The guy was watching me. At one point he leaned forward and pointed through the dome and said, "The gentleman drinking beside the diving board. Hemingway."

Hemingway was fat and bloated. He looked like I could take him out easy and drink him under the table.

I said, "And the blonde talking to Hemingway?"

"That's Samantha Dennison, a poet working in the mid twenty-first century. Would you care to meet her?"

"Sure. Bring her over."

He hesitated, then got up and left the bar. I watched him cross to Hemingway and the blonde and murmur something to them. The blonde looked up, squinting against the sunlight. She nodded, said something to Papa, and walked back with the guy.

I raised my bottle at Hemingway and he smiled and saluted me with his glass.

The blonde had style, the way she walked in and folded herself into the chair and held out a hand. "Mr. Bukowski," she said.

I nodded. "Drink?"

She looked at her glass. It was empty. She said, "G&T."

The guy stood up and hurried to the bar and came back with a drink. She sipped and looked at me and said, "Have you been here long, Mr. Bukowski?"

"A day, and that's a day too long."

She smiled. "You'll get used to the place," she said. "We all do."

I took another shot of Daniels and leaned forward and said, "You're a very beautiful woman."

Her smile faltered. "Why, thank–"

"You and Hemingway down there. You together?"

She said, "We're friends, Mr. Bukowski."

I leaned forward, swaying a little, the Jack Daniels on top of all that sun. I said, "You put out, Samantha?"

"Excuse me?"

"I said, do you fuck?" I said.

"What–"

"How'd you like to come back to my place for a quick fuck?"

She said to the guy, "Did you say Mr. Bukowski hails from the dark ages, Max?"

The guy – Max – he said, "Mr. Bukowski was writing in the latter half of the twentieth century, Samantha."

"Writing what?"

Max said, "Poetry, short stories, novels."

"Poetry? I find that hard to believe."

I was losing it and all I wanted to do was get her in the sack. I looked from her perfect face to her big, perfect breasts.

She said, "You are somewhat primitive, Mr. Bukowski."

She stood and strode from the bar.

"And you," I called after her, "you're one sassy round-heeled little cunt!"

I sat and drank. The sun moved across the sky. I finished my quart and I was sweating. I missed Jane. At one point I turned to the guy, Max, and I said, "Take me to a whorehouse, Max."

"I'm afraid, Mr. Bukowski, that we don't have such establishments on Mars."

"What kind of place is this?" I yelled.

I sweated and drank and I was feeling bad. I thought about LA. I thought about Jane and all the arguments and all the drinking and the all fucking and I missed her.

I said to Max, "I want to go back to Earth, Max."

"I'm afraid that's impossible, Mr. Bukowski."

"Why impossible? You bring me back to life. You bring Papa and all us fucking so-called greats back to life. What's a little rocket trip back to Earth?"

He looked at me. "The Earth doesn't exist anymore, Mr. Bukowski. We managed to extract a few thousand DNA samples before the last war–"

"Doesn't exist?"

"The planet was annihilated in the Fourth global conflict."

I looked into the twilit sky, looking for Earth. All I could see were the first of the stars coming out.

I stood up and knocked over the table and staggered towards the exit. Max was at my side. He took my arm and I felt like swinging for him but I just said, "Doesn't exist..." and he guided me back to the dome.

I got myself a beer and he left. I sat by the wall and stared out across the red sands.

I thought about LA and the races and Mulholland Drive and Macarthur Park and the Post Office where I worked my ass to death and I thought about Jane and Barbara and Frances and Linda and all my other women and the other good souls I knew, and Bob the editor at Black Sparrow Press, who saved my life when he got me out of the Post Office and gave me enough to allow me to write.

And I drained the bottle and smashed it on the floor tiles so I had a nice long shard like a blade, and I stretched out my left arm and cut it, not across the wrist like a fairy but real good, from the wrist upwards to the inside of the elbow, slicing the length of the vein, like a man. Blood flowed bright, lots of it, and I passed out laughing.

"Wake up, Buk!"

I opened my eyes and sat up.

Max was smiling down at me.

"How are you feeling, Buk?"

I looked at my arm. The scar was healed. I was okay, a bit of a hangover was all.

He said, "You can't do things like that, Buk."

"Get me a beer."

He got me a beer from the cooler and I drank.

The sun was up and the desert outside was red. There was no one about and that was fine by me.

I said, "What do you want me to do?" and I hated the note of pleading in my voice.

He said, "Write about Earth, Buk."

He left and I sat in the chair and stared out of the dome. I opened a beer and drank.

Later that day he came by with an upright Remington and a ream of quarto, then left without a word.

I drank all day and around about ten that evening I sat at the desk in front of the Remington and I wound in a sheet of paper and reached for a beer and began typing.

10.03, in my dome, on Mars.

# People of Planet Earth

*I normally write quiet SF about nice, respectable people. The last story doesn't really fit into that category, and nor does this one. I don't often write about alien invasion, and never about anal sex, and I've no idea where the idea to combine the two came from. I do know that from time to time I despair of the human race – which has led to my writing novels like Kéthani and The Serene Invasion, in which aliens come to Earth in order to help us out.*

That night, during sex, I crawled up Jasper Wentworth's anus.

Until then the sex had been routine, a mere tired playing out of rote moves and roles. Jasper had accused me of not being committed. I was remote, he said, distant. I made no effort to get to know him, he claimed, to get under his skin.

"I think you don't love me, Eve."

Panicked, I reassured him that I did. "You mean the world to me," I said. I didn't want to lose what I had with him – or what I would have.

We'd met in a trendy club in a side street not far from Westminster. It was the fashionable haunt of the latest intake of young opposition MPs who had no qualms about snorting coke from the marble surfaces of the club's luxurious toilets in the early hours, and later in the day denouncing pushers from the floor of the House.

I was on a high stool at the bar, waiting for him when he walked in with a brunette on his arm.

I caught his eye, smiled, and the woman didn't stand a chance.

He shrugged her off a little later and we talked. He was impressed, like the chauvinist he was, with my knowledge of politics. Impressed, too, and flattered, that I should know so much about his illustrious career.

I told him I was new in town, which was no lie, and that I worked in futures... which was also the truth, of sorts. He was intrigued, and lustful, and I knew I'd caught my man.

I dragged him back to my apartment and made sure he'd be back the next night. I never cease to be amazed at how predictable is the male of the species. All that was required of me to keep him interested was the requisite gymnastic contortions, with concomitant moaning and *faux* orgasm, and the promise of more to come. Afterwards he slept like a babe while I considered the future.

Over the next couple of weeks, the pillow talk flowed. His dreams and desires, his ambitions. He had his eye on a cabinet post when his party was elected to power next year, as seemed likely. He reckoned he would be the PM within a year.

I massaged his ego, this tall fair country boy, scion of the Wentworths of Shropshire, Eton- and Oxford-educated. He was bright, without question, and arrogant, and ambitious, and these attributes made for a lethal combination.

"You're a strange woman, Eve," he said one night.

"Strange?"

"I've never met anyone quite like you. You have an ineluctable quality – charm and allure... and yet a certain coldness."

I thought, but did not say, that he was intimidated by my intellect. Men of his type always are.

"You know so much, and yet lack..."

"What?" I insisted.

He shook his head, and changed the subject. He had been about to say: humanity.

I introduced him to the pleasures of anal manipulation two months into our relationship. For a man of the world, he was relatively inexperienced in bed. He knew what he wanted, and presumed therefore he knew what women wanted. He would lap dutifully till I faked delight, then kneel and ease himself into me. From then on it was a matter of his thrusting away until he came... or frequently failed to do so.

I began by rimming his rectum with a saliva'd forefinger, gently kneading, easing open the sphincter, then inserting the finger up to its hilt, feeling the silken membrane slick with rectal mucus, timing my thrusts to his frantic penile bargings.

He moaned and came in torrents, and later looked at me with increased respect.

He began to rely on my probings. He insisted I digitally bugger him every night, and soon I was playing variations on the theme, inserting two fingers, then three, then five – upping the tempo until he was a delirious glove-puppet to my aggressive fistings. In time he failed to come without my forearm buried up to the elbow.

And when he was in the throes delirium, and I heady with power, I wondered what his constituency members, his parliamentary colleagues, would make of his lack of decorum.

He liked to reminisce, post-coitally, about the night we met.

"I should have known, Eve, that my life was about to change. It was a harbinger, a sign that great things were about to happen."

I assured him that it was.

He was speaking about the meteorite he'd witnessed over west London. On the terrace at Westminster with a gaggle of back-benchers, he'd looked up to see a diamond scoring the night sky, a bright point of light sliding down over Knightsbridge.

It was an indication of his ego that he thought it right that the meteorite should descend over his very own constituency.

"And that very night you walked into my life, Eve."

We had been together three months when he accused me of erecting an emotional *cordon sanitaire*, of being remote, even cold. He said I was not the least concerned about him as a person, about his feelings and emotions, and wanted him only for sex.

I worked to ease his concerns, and took more interest in his ambitions. I probed his mind with all the diligence that, alone in his flat, I probed his derrière.

He was moving up in the party, manoeuvring himself with all the mendacity of his kind to take advantage of the imminent downfall of a colleague. He was a favourite of the leader, soon to stand down, and popular with fellow back-benchers. With the approach of the election, some newspapers were talking of him as the next white hope, the dashing blade with looks, charm and brains.

He threw himself into work, and I worked at throwing myself into him.

Long into the earlier hours, at mid-point in sweaty bouts of sex, I eased two hands into his anus, then pressed palms together in simulated prayer and thrust forward, as if reaching for his heart. After a month of similar exercise, I could part his sphincter wide enough to allow the entry of my head. I was adept at holding my breath for long minutes, and this helped as his elastic rectal membrane shrink-wrapped around my face. I head-fucked him every night for a week, and then prepared for the insertion of my shoulders.

I feigned adoration, love. I had never felt anything but contempt for him, as I came to understand how shallow he was, how self-centred, how mendacious. He craved power and would stop at nothing to get it.

My dissimulation was a small price to pay for the ultimate reward.

He liked to tell me of his vaulting ambitions as we lay panting after sex, my hair sodden, redolent with his visceral fluids.

He toed the party line, but would change things incrementally when in power. He would cover the nation's blushes over Syria with the invasion of Iran, with a slew of base nationalistic policies designed to woo a bovine electorate.

I listened to him, and smiled, and he took my smile as willing complicity, even endorsement.

That night, a month before the general election, as he was on all fours on the bed and I worked on his rear, it came to me suddenly that now was the time.

He was a carcass, a moaning slab of meat wracked with ecstasy, as I eased my palms between his cheeks, and parted, then slid my head, then my shoulders, into his colonic cavern. The pulse of his heartbeat throbbed in my ears, quickening as he came in cataracts and screamed in a paroxysm of euphoria. I too felt elation, as I neared my goal, as I palmed aside faecal matter and then the semi-digested content of his lower intestines. I thrust my head, allowed my shoulders to open out, expanding his containing flesh. I was laughing mentally, maniacally, as I pulled my knees up through his closing sphincter and slipped into him as if donning a new suit, inhabiting him completely.

I spread myself, taking delight in how well he fitted.

I rolled from the bed, gained my feet, totally in control now. I stretched, testing new muscles, luxuriating in his flesh. It was an exhilarating sensation to inhabit at last a male member of the species, commander of his superb physique, keeper of his memories, heir to his power.

I padded over to the mirror and stared at my new self.

I was aware of his slowly fading mentation, asking: *Why?*

His face twitched with a desperate effort at resistance, but I exerted power and gained mastery of his features.

I smiled at him, at myself.

"Where I come from," I said, "we do things differently. And you *do* need help."

A year later, at the despatch box, I smiled across at the shadow benches and awaited my moment. The day before I had consulted my colleagues around the globe, powerful figures in government and business, leaders of the world religions, for the latter had proved to be just as corrupt and malign.

Now I was to outline the co-ordinated policies that would unite world leaders and usher in a new order of social enlightenment.

"Ladies and gentlemen, Speaker of the House..."

The opposition ranks listened, spellbound, such was my allure.

And as I smiled, I thought how I despised these creatures, how I loathed these upstart apes driven by base instincts of ego and power and greed… and how I pitied them, also.

And I laughed, inwardly, at the irony of my species' humanising the people of planet Earth.

# P.O.O.C.H.

*Only when I came to collate the stories for this collection did I realise that they share a common theme. They are all in some way about strangers or visitors coming to Earth (or to Mars) – and in two instances travelling to a far future Earth. In some of the stories the visitors come of their own volition, in others they are brought to the locale in question for various reasons. In the following story the visitor or stranger is neither human nor alien, but a dog. It's one of the most autobiographical tales I've written, as against my strenuous objections the two ladies of my life, my wife and daughter, somehow persuaded me that the addition of a dog to the family would be an asset. So we bought a red and white setter puppy and for a month or so my life was hell. (And still is, occasionally – like now, as Uther is jumping up at my keyboard and zxcdfvghjuikocvfgbhujikop... demanding he be allowed to help write this introduction.) It was a short leap of the imagination to conceive of a future where convicts were not imprisoned but given a dog...*

In my defence I must say that I thought of my crime as victimless. I don't consider banks to be victims, and I didn't hack into their data bases in order to line my own pockets. I simply entered the accounts of a few millionaires and shifted a small amount of cash, every day for a year, to the accounts of various charitable organisations.

"You'll be lucky to get less than two years," my lawyer told me before the verdict was announced. "They'll make an example of you."

"Two years..." I said. "Do they let you have laptops inside?"

She gave me a withering look. "You know your trouble, Mr Rice? You don't get out enough."

"Outside's overrated."

"Or meet enough people."

"People ditto," I said.

She sighed. "Mr Rice, may I ask you if you have any friends?"

I avoided her eyes. "Thousands..."

"I meant in the *real* world."

"Define the 'real world'."

She smiled with satisfaction. "I'll take that as no."

"Actually..." I said.

"Yes?"

I stared at the concrete floor of the holding cell. Actually... she was right.

I did have a friend, once. Billy, a mate from primary school. We had the same interests from the start, a fascination with everything computer related: we grew up on Sinclair Spectrums, then Amstrads, then PCs... right up to the latest Hayakawa virtual rigs... And then Billy jumped off Beachy Head without even leaving a note – online or otherwise.

She reached out and laid a hand on mine. I pulled my hand away. "Mr Rice, Michael, take my advice. When all this is over, meet people, join clubs, travel."

I heard footsteps outside the cell and the duty Sergeant bellowed. "Rice!"

"Good luck, Michael."

I trudged from the cell without replying.

I was ready for whatever the bastards wanted to throw at me. Two years, five – it was all the same to me. I'd find it hard to live without my laptop, but I'd been on remand for a month without a sniff of a PC and I'd survived. After a fashion.

I glanced across at the jury, and to a man and woman they avoided my gaze.

Which wasn't all that reassuring.

The judge summed up, called me a danger to civilised society, and went on, "In normal circumstances I would have little hesitation in passing the maximum sentence available to me. However..." He glanced at the softscreen before him, pulled a distasteful face, and went on, "However, after consulting various experts in the matter I have been advised that a sentence of six months correctional surveillance will suffice."

I stared at him in amazement, followed by relief.

I didn't have the slightest idea what 'correctional surveillance' might mean – but I found out soon enough.

"P.O.O.C.H.," the handler said, holding the leash of a slavering hound. The animal was on its hind legs, straining to get at me. "Personal

Omni-Operational Correctional Hound," he explained.

And then he released the dog.

I flinched, expecting to feel its teeth sink into my arm. Instead, a wet tongue laundered my face. I collapsed under the weight of the beast as it pawed me like a deranged heavyweight boxer.

"Down, boy," the handler said, and instantly the dog retreated and sat on its haunches, panting, a foot-long tongue lolling over the battlements of its teeth.

"Pooch is programmed to respond to my instructions," the handler said, "but on hand-over I'll wipe its operating system and install the correctional program. Then it will be up to you to attend to its training. As part of your correctional therapy you must attend obedience classes once a week for six months."

I stared at the dog. "You... you mean, it isn't real? I mean, it isn't a dog?"

The handler smiled. "Pooch is a robot, but a very advanced specimen. Inside the biological tegument is an integrated parallel processing smartcore."

I stared at the drool lacing its lips, at its bright eyes staring at me. I sniffed. It even smelled like a dog. "Amazing."

"It'll be your constant companion, Mr Rice, for the next six months."

I could hardly contain my delight. "I don't know what to say," I said. "I expected at least two years."

The handler smiled to himself. "And by the end of the six months," he murmured, "you'll be begging to be banged up."

The handler passed me the lead, along with an instructional DVD, and said I was free to go.

"You mean... I can just walk out of here? Walk out... a free man?"

That knowing smile again. "Off you go, Mr Rice."

I needed no further encouragement. I took the lead and walked from the magistrate's court. Or perhaps I should rephrase that: I was tugged headfirst from the court by a combined bulldozer, express train and whirlwind incarnated in the form of a canine. I was hauled along the pavement at high speed, my arm almost parting company with its socket. No degree of force on my part was sufficient to slow the beast down, and no cried commands to halt had the desired effect.

Passers-by stopped and stared as I was yanked on a slalom rush between them; children laughed and pointed. When we reached the end of the road, I admit I closed my eyes. I could imagine the headlines: Hound Hauls Hacker in Hit-and-Run Horror.

I opened my eyes when the expected flesh-and-metal impact failed to eventuate.

Pooch sat on the curb, as innocent as a guide dog. When a suitable gap appeared in the traffic, he trotted across the road with all the nonchalance of a Cruft's Best of Breed winner... and then took off on the other side.

I cried out loud, held onto the lead, and was hauled across Finsbury Park and along Blackstock Road towards the crumbling Victorian pile where I had my bed-sit.

At the sanctuary of my palatial abode – I'm employing irony here – I expected respite. I was sadly disappointed.

I collapsed onto my sofa – and Pooch jumped on top of me, half a hundredweight of slavering hound with halitosis from Hell.

He jumped down and ran across the room to the fridge, looked at me pleadingly and, when I failed to respond, returned and grabbed the cuff of my jumper between his incisors and dragged me across the room.

I got the message. The hound was hungry.

In the freezer I found an old pizza, a pack of burgers and three frankfurters. I defrosted and cooked them, then watched as Pooch devoured the impromptu meal with more noise than a faulty waste disposal unit. And I thought I had bad table manners.

After the meal, and to my vast relief, Pooch turned in a circle on the rug, round and round as if trying to lap his own tale, then suddenly and without warning fell to the ground.

He farted, then began snoring. Pooch was asleep.

I took the opportunity to insert the DVD into the wallscreen, then sat back and watched. I even celebrated my dubious freedom with a can of Carling.

"Personal Omni-Operational Correctional Hounds – or Pooch for short," said a saccharine voice-over as a hound identical to my own

Pooch cavorted across a field in pursuit of a Frisbee, "is in appearance, behaviour and temperament identical to a real, living, flesh and blood dog. In this instance, Pooch's operating programme has been styled on the characteristics of a Setter, a breed known for its agility, speed and affection. This short program will tell you everything you need to know about your Pooch, your responsibilities towards it, and the terms and conditions of your custody."

I watched, with growing horror, as the full meaning of my punishment was played out before me.

Pooch would require three long – an hour at least – walks a day.

Pooch would require a pound of minced steak and half a pound of dry biscuits per day – as well as supernumerary treats.

Pooch would be in attendance twenty-four hours a day.

Pooch would lavish upon its 'owner' all the affection of a real dog.

I watched, appalled, as the voiceover described eating habits, toileting, training and sundry other minutiae I had not even dreamed might accompany the owning of a dog. As the credits rolled over the shot of the hound leaping to snatch the Frisbee from the air, the doorbell rang and I leapt to answer to summons before it awoke the sleeping hound.

A deliveryman and assistant stood on the threshold with half a dozen parcels. "Michael Rice? These are from the correctional facility. If you'd just sign here..."

Five minutes later I unpacked a doggy basket the size of a bath, various feeding bowls, grooming paraphernalia, spare leads and, last but not least, something described in an accompanying leaflet as a poop-wand – an electrically powered column which hoovered up doggy excrement and stored it in a small reservoir which had to be emptied daily.

I'd barely read the operating instructions of this last item when I heard an almighty yawn. Pooch rose to his full height, stretched limb by limb, and trotted to the door. He stared at me with big eyes, then gave vent to a noxious alimentary blast.

I was about to test the efficacy of the poop-wand.

The following evening I attended my first obedience class. It was held at Finsbury Park community centre and was run by a woman who resembled a St. Bernard with the hectoring manner of a sadistic Sergeant Major.

Twenty hounds and their owners filled the hall, and I'd never imagined – not that I'd ever given the subject much thought – that the descendent of the wolf could have diverged into so many disparate forms. There were Chihuahuas and Poodles, Labradors and Retrievers, Daschunds and Dobermans, as well as a dozen mutts of unspecified parentage. And their owners were almost as various, young and old, men and women... though there was a marked absence of men of my own age – late-twenties. Ah, the wisdom of relative youth.

Pooch raced around the hall in a paroxysm of canine meet-and-greet that left me exhausted. He pawed and sniffed and nipped and rolled, licked genitalia and had his own inspected and tongued... As far as I was aware, he was the only POOCH on parade, and he seemed to pass the sniff-test with flying colours.

"Now your dog," began the Sergeant Majoress, "is not a human. Obvious, you might think – but many people make the mistake of assuming that their dog thinks like a human being. Instead, consider your precious hound an alien. They are pack animals, and in a pack of dogs there is something called a pecking order. It is vital that your dog understands that you, its owner, are at the very apex of that pecking order – and over the course of the next few weeks I'll ensure that you know how to establish this fact. Now, we'll begin with a few basic commands."

And so it went. I learned how to make Pooch sit and stand and lie down and wait and come... which he did, intermittently, while at other times he seemed to take great delight in ignoring me.

"Persevere, Mr Rice!" she said as she did the rounds. "You'll soon get the hang of it."

One hour later I was near complete exhaustion and Pooch seemed game for another hour. At one point we had to exchange pets, and I passed Pooch into the custody of a buxom girl in a Star Quest gaming tee-shirt.

"Nice shirt," I said as I took custody of her miniscule whippet.

"Nice setter," she said as she wrestled, with more success than I'd been having, with Pooch. "You like gaming?" she went on.

I coloured to the roots of my admittedly thinning hair. "Addicted to it," I said.

"Every played Lyran Attack?"

"Played it? I almost live the game. Level twenty," I said, preening.

Her eyes goggled. "Twenty? Gosh! We must..." she began, before Pooch hauled her halfway across the hall.

I arrived back at my bed-sit at ten, wrung-out, exhausted – and not much the wiser viz the training of dogs...

I awoke in the morning when what felt like a rhinoceros dropped onto my bed. Pooch proceeded to give me a bed-bath with his tongue. I groaned and reached for my bedside clock. I groaned again. Six o'clock!

Then I sniffed.

Either the toilet had backed up and the entire content of the London sewer had found its ways into the bed-sit, or the mechanical menace that was Pooch had discharged last night's supper onto the bedroom carpet.

I suspected the latter, and was proven correct when I rolled out of bed and planted my bare foot on something soft, warm, and very, very smelly.

"You bastard!" I wailed, and hopped to the bathroom.

Let me tell you something about my daily routine before I was stupid enough to have Pooch blight my life.

I'd rise about eleven, shower, then make my way to the local greasy spoon. Breakfast for an hour – full English, of course – then back to my place for a serious session on the PC. For the next few hours I'd be online, snacking on the occasional take-away and refuelling with strong coffee. I'd rather keep what I did during those hours online confidential, of course; once bitten, etc... Around six I'd fix myself a pizza or call out for an Indian take-away. From then until midnight I'd be online again, either gaming or saving the world. Two days a week I'd do a little software programming or web design in order to bring in some cash and keep body and soul together.

All in all I led a pretty satisfying existence. Not everyone's pot of Earl Grey, I admit, but I wasn't complaining.

Pooch changed all that.

And how.

I became a slave.

He imposed a routine upon my existence that did not sit well with my body clock. To stop him fouling the bed-sit I had to get up at six and take him for a long walk – a short trip to the local park for a quick squat was not sufficient; he demanded a trek: two miles minimum. On the way back he allowed me to stop off at the café to consume a quick breakfast – he allotted me fifteen minutes before tugging at the lead and demanding we return home. There I commenced a ten minute training session, gave him a biscuit and, when he'd settled down, tiptoed over to my PC and did a couple of hours 'work'. Lunchtime brought another two mile walk followed by more training and then lunch. According to the DVD I was top dog in this household and was therefore expected to eat before Pooch, which I did... all the while being watched by a pair of rheumy eyes that engendered in me a ridiculous sense of guilt.

He allowed me an hour after lunch to do a little more at the PC before he commenced to make my life a misery by:

Jumping up while I was at the PC and pawing the keyboard...

Being suspiciously quiet for five minutes, which soon alerted me to the fact that he was up to mischief: either chewing something he was not allowed to chew – electric cable, books and magazines, shoes and slippers – or rooting in the litter bin for scraps of food or plastic containers he liked to chomp on.

Defecating/urinating on the carpet when I was two minutes late in taking him out for his afternoon constitutional.

Howling at me to demand we play tug-of-war...

I was a peaceable man by nature, but he soon brought out the Mr Hyde in me – and I was not proud of the anger I exhibited towards the animal at these times, and always fell into a slough of self-loathing guilt soon after.

One afternoon, a week after Pooch entered my life, I was attempting to annihilate a platoon of invading extraterrestrials, in order to reach level thirty of Lyran Attack!, when a preternatural quiet set my mental alarm bells clanging. I looked around the room and saw Pooch, in the hall, eating something.

"No!" I cried in rage and despair. I bolted from my swivel chair and charged into the hall, grunting like a sumo wrestler on steroids.

"You utter, utter fucking bastard!"

He looked up at me with huge caramel eyes, as if butter would melt in his muzzle, the masticated shreds of my entire 2000AD comic collection strewn across the carpet.

I fell to my knees and wept, then lashed out and backhanded his head. He yelped and scuttled off, cowering by the door.

Gathering up the remains of my prized collection, I shuffled to the kitchen and dumped them in the bin. "You bastard..." I wept, and I might have been meaning myself.

My late nights at the keyboard were a thing of the past. He demanded a walk at ten o'clock, after which I was too exhausted to do anything other than fall into bed at the unfeasibly early hour of eleven. Then up at six the following morning.

I looked into the future and despaired. I had another five and a half months of this hell to endure.

Meanwhile, the obedience classes continued, for the little good they did. Pooch had mastered the basic commands of 'sit' and 'down' – but he was entirely selective as to when he chose to obey.

"That's your fault, Mr Rice," said the Sergeant Majoress. "You must issue you commands with authority."

"Authority? I don't think I do authority."

"Like this," she said, and bellowed at Pooch as he leapt up at me. "Down, Pooch!"

He dropped like the proverbial felled heavyweight. She gave him a treat

"There. Now you try."

When he stood on his hind legs and pawed at my face, I shouted, "Down, Pooch," and he dropped, albeit with reluctance.

The Sergeant Majoress smiled. "You're getting there, Mr Rice."

"Except, when he leaves this place he'll just ignore me as usual."

"Then you must persevere, Mr Rice. Little and often, little and often. You'll soon get the hang!"

Later, while I was leading Pooch around the hall – or rather while he was dragging me around the hall – he decided to squat and void a noxious smelling dollop. "You little..." I hissed, employing my poop-wand and disinfecting the area with spray.

Exhausted, I collapsed on a bucket chair at the end of the hall.

Someone came and sat next to me. It was the big girl in the Star

Quest tee-shirt.

She smiled sympathetically. "You looked pooped."

"Ha, ha."

"Oh, I didn't mean..."

I stared at the dog, now curled at my feet like a paragon of virtue.

I sighed. "He's killing me. I'm beat. You wouldn't believe..."

"Finding it hard work?"

"Hard? I never imagined... He's *wrecked* my life. Ruined it. I had a routine, *my* routine... Now all that's gone. It's all about *him*, *him*, *him*... Why do sane people willingly have dogs is what I'd like to know."

She looked from me to her anorexic whippet, licking itself at her feet. "Why did you get Pooch?" she asked.

I opened my mouth, closed it, and thought furiously. "Ah," I said, "It was a rescue dog. I mean, a friend got it... But – but he died, threw himself off a cliff. So..." I shrugged. "So I took him in."

"And you're beginning to regret it?"

"You bet. And you know what? You know what the worse thing is?"

"Having your routine disrupted?" she said in a half-censorious tone as if she resented my shallowness.

"No. Well, that's bad enough. But worse than that is... Well, when I get angry, and yell at him and... and hit out. Not that I actually hit him, of course. But the desire is there..." I shrugged. "And then the guilt. I don't like myself, then. I don't like the side of me that *he's* brought out."

She smiled at me. "People get to know themselves when they own a dog," she said. "It's like any form of relationship, I suppose. You get to know the other person *and* yourself." She held out a hand. "I'm Maxine, by the way."

I took her hand, briefly. "Michael."

She told me about her dog – Sandy the whippet – and how she'd bought it soon after her mum had passed away. "Not that I was looking for a replacement," she hastened to add. "But I looked after Mum for five years while she was ill, and when she died... Well, there was a big gap."

*So you filled it with a dog*, I thought; *how sad.*

"Still playing Lyran Attack!?" The question interrupted my reverie on the insanity of dog-owners.

"Level twenty-two," I boasted.

"Impressive." She stared at me. "Hey, have you been to the Virtorium on the High Street?"

"What? With *him*?" I gestured at Pooch.

"If you make sure he's well fed, then take him on a long walk, I'm sure he'll settle down for an hour or so, allow you to play a little. I take Sandy along a couple of times a week."

I shifted on the bucket-seat, uncomfortable at where this might be leading.

"Hey, Michael, why don't we meet up at the Virtorium? I'll show you the place. We could..."

"I wouldn't feel confident taking Pooch, just yet." I saw disappointment in her eyes, so to soften the blow I offered, "Look, why don't we meet up online? There's a hot site I've just found, we could virt-game one to one."

She smiled. "That sounds great."

And so began our – virtual – relationship.

Meanwhile, Pooch continued to rule my life.

I don't know what was the worst; the long walks he demanded three times a day or his continual sentry-like presence in the bed-sit. The walks took three great chunks out of my day, and I returned home feeling physically shattered, my wrist-, elbow- and shoulder-joints throbbing with pain from being almost dislocated by Pooch's incessant yanking on the extendible lead – which was an aggravation in itself. The hound wound in and out of trees on the heath while the lead was on full extension, and of course when entangled could not find his own way back: this necessitated my following him, cursing and swearing, around trees and through undergrowth, often snagging myself in the process. I must have provided a great source of amusement for passers-by blessed by the state of being dogless.

And when I returned home, the torment – of a different kind – continued. Here Pooch insisted on following me from hall to kitchen to bed-sitting room, never taking his gaze from me. He chose the most inopportune times to yelp at the door, which meant that he needed to be released for a pee. He chewed everything chewable that was not placed beyond his reach. He interrupted my work by slapping his great paws on the keyboard. He drove me insensate with rage.

At one point, an hour into entering code for a website I'd been commissioned to design, Pooch ambled across to me, stared into my eyes, and then, without warning, launched himself into my lap – dragging his feet across the keyboard in a rattling arpeggio that also just happened to erase the page I'd been working on.

"You bastard!" I cried – and as he leapt back in alarm, I attacked him.

I rolled from the chair and dived at the dog, grabbed him by the throat and wrestled him to the ground. He yipped as I pinned him to the rug with all my considerable weight. He tried to nip me and I struck his head. "You *bastard*! Don't bite!"

I pressed him to the ground, rendering him immobile. His chest heaved. He panted. The eye closest to me swivelled, regarding me with fear.

"You. Do. Not. Jump. Up. While. I. Am. WORKING!"

Then I released him and struggled to my feet. Pooch scuttled off and curled himself into a corner, casting me reproachful glances as I resumed my seat.

I felt a second's cathartic satisfaction, followed by the gnawing knowledge that what I'd done was both useless in terms of discipline, and damaging to both me and the dog.

I recalled a line from the instructional DVD. *The use of force against your charge is futile; in the wild, alpha males do not dominate with displays of brutality, but by alternative means of leadership: instruction, perseverance, and oral commands.*

Which, of course, made me resent the animal all the more.

The *animal*, I thought to myself. The thing was so lifelike in every respect that I thought of it as an animal. I told myself that it was a machine – a very complex machine, granted, but a machine all the same. What I'd done to it could not be considered cruelty, I told myself: how could you be cruel to a non-sentient, unthinking machine...?

For some reason, however, I still felt bad about my involuntary violent outburst.

That night, for a couple of hours, between Pooch's evening walk and his last trot around the block for a pee, I played Lyran Attack! with Maxine.

She'd proved a stiff opponent in the past, though I'd always managed to overcome her in the end. Tonight, however, she beat me hands down six games running and progressed to level twenty-five in the process.

In the chat-room afterwards, she said: What was wrong with you tonight?

Me: Nothing. I'm fine. Well done.

Maxine: How's Pooch?

Me: Don't ask.

Maxine: Like that, hm?

Me: He's driving me nuts.

Maxine: Hang in there.

Across the room, Pooch climbed to his feet, stretched, then trotted to the door and yipped to be taken out.

Me: I'd better go. He wants his last thing at night walkies...

Maxine: See you tomorrow night at O class.

Me: See you there.

I logged out, sighed, and fetched the lead.

The strange thing was that I liked meeting Maxine in the virtual world of Lyran Attack!, and enjoyed chatting with her afterwards, but I was uneasy talking to her at obedience classes.

I've always found being around people hard work. I find responding difficult; I mean, I have things to say, sometimes, but it's replying to what others say to me that I find hard to judge. I either make the wrong response, and get odd looks or cold silences, or I'm unable to respond at all. It's as if my brain freezes, unable to process data, leaving me stranded and feeling even more isolated and inadequate than ever.

It wasn't so bad with Maxine, but even so some of the things she said left me uncomfortable and embarrassed and floundering in silence.

That night, during a break in the lesson, I asked her about the Lyran Attack! film that came out last year. I told her it stank, from the crass opening credits onwards, and she responded: "Oh, well, I liked it."

I blinked. "What was to like?"

"Well, okay, I agree the plot was nothing, and the *deus ex machina*...

well that was laughable – and insulting to a half intelligent audience. But I thought the characterisation, for a sci-fi action film, well done."

I stared at her. "The characterisation?" I tried to recall the characterisation... I couldn't even remember the characters, never mind anything that might have characterised them.

"Johnny and Zelda – their relationship?" she stared at me as if I were dummy.

"Oh, that... It was irrelevant to the story."

"Irrelevant?" She laughed. "Michael, it was what the story was *about*, for heaven's sake."

Silence from me. Then: "*It was?* But I thought..."

"The entire conceit of the attack was brought about by Johnny's inability to commit... You didn't get that?"

I coloured and shook my head and retreated into embarrassed silence.

I was saved by the Sergeant Majoress who called us, and our dogs, to order.

At the end of the night Maxine came up to me and said. "Michael, Lyran Attack! 2 is showing at the multiplex on Saturday... I'd like to see it. Why not come along? I'll explain what you don't understand..."

I looked away from her smiling face, said, "I'm doing something that night," and hurried from the hall after Pooch.

I walked home across the park, surrounded by strolling couples and groups of kids hanging out, laughing and shouting, and battled with a small voice in my head that said that I should have taken up Maxine's invitation.

I attacked Pooch again a few days later.

I'd ordered an early edition of Alan Moore's classic *V for Vendetta* from Amazon a week earlier, and it arrived on Thursday morning.

Pooch got to the letterbox before me.

By the time I arrived, he'd chewed through the envelope and turned half the comic to sopping pulp.

I lost it, went berserk, and kicked the beast.

He hit the door, yipping in pain, and I kicked him again – then fled sobbing into the bathroom.

He followed me: he'd succeeded in breaking the bolt on the

bathroom door a day after he arrived. Now he stood on the threshold, watching me with his vast liquid eyes, accusing me and at the same time beseeching, as I sat on the side of the bath with my head in my hands and wept.

"You bastard," I said, over and over. "You utter bastard..."

I missed the obedience class the following week. The day after, unable to take any more, I snapped and came to a decision. My life had changed irrevocably for the worst. I was imprisoned in my own home by a routine and a responsibility that was crippling me. I had to do something about it.

That afternoon I took Pooch on a long walk around Finsbury Park. I watched the busses pass along Blackstock Road, one every few minutes, and timed their passing to my walk around the perimeter of the park. Then, as the number 19 grumbled to halt at the stop and a queue of people shuffled aboard, I tied Pooch by his lead to a tree and ran for the bus, jumping aboard a second before the doors concertinaed shut.

I took my seat – Pooch was staring at me as the bus pulled off into the traffic – and looked away.

I rode the bus for a mile, then got off and found a café. I ordered a latte and two chocolate muffins and relished the thirty minutes of reprieve.

Thirty minute because, as I looked up after scraping the remains of the second muffin from its case with my teeth, who should come trotting around the corner but the hound himself, the remains of his bitten-through lead trailing along the pavement behind him.

Holding back tears of despair, I picked up the shortened lead and led him in silence to the bus stop.

As soon as I got back I found the number of the magistrate's helpline from the DVD and put through a call. "I need help. I can't cope. I swear, I'll... I'll either disable the... the *machine*, or... or I'll...."

The upshot was that they agreed, twenty minutes later when a soft-voiced woman had talked me into a state of comparative calm, to send round a counsellor at ten the following morning.

I returned to the bed-sit at nine forty-five in the morning, after giving the dog its first walk of the day, and five minutes later the doorbell sounded.

"You're early," I said as I pulled open the door. "Oh," I went on, surprised – it was Maxine. "Ah, I'm sorry, Maxine. I'm... I'm expecting someone at any minute."

She just stared at me, smiling.

"So... well," I stammered. "See you at the next obedience class."

She stopped me from closing the door. "Michael," she said hurriedly, "why do you think I'm here?"

My face burned. "Ah..." Then I realised. "Oh, the copy of Martian Trek I told you about..." I began with relief.

"You can be silly sometimes, Michael. I'm here to counsel you about your Personal Omni-Operational Correctional Hound," she said.

I just stood there, holding the door with one hand, staring at her with my mouth hanging open.

"You... Excuse me. What did you say?"

She repeated herself, then went on, "Now, perhaps if you'd let me in...?"

"You... you're the counsellor?" I said stupidly, still clutching the door.

"Yes, Michael. Now..." She opened her eyes even wider and stared at me quizzically.

I stood back and Maxine entered. I looked behind her. "No Sandy?"

She avoided my eyes. "No. No, Sandy."

Uncomfortable beyond description, I led Maxine inside and indicated the sofa. She sat down, staring around at the mess I call home, taking in the drifts of comics, the empty pizza boxes and crushed take-away foil trays. Strange, but I'd never before realised what a dump it was.

I thought about Maxine, and the phone call, and her presence at the obedience class...

And I suddenly felt indignant.

"I get it," I said, slumping into an armchair after first removing a pile of graphic novels. "The class, you... Very clever. Big Brother. The nanny state and all that."

She stared at me. "Michael, what on Earth are you talking about?"

"You, being at the obedience classes. I realise now that it was just too coincidental... You're a mole, sent there to monitor my progress, right?"

All those hours we'd spent online, duelling on the regolith of Lunar, all the chats afterwards... and her invitation to the film that time.

All part of her daily work.

A part of me that I kept closed up and locked away felt... felt oddly cheated. Then I slammed the door shut again and told myself that this was only to be expected. I was a criminal, after all, and the authorities had a responsibility to keep tabs on those on P.O.O.C.H. parole like myself.

She drew a big sigh. "Michael, you've got it wrong."

"But you said you were a counsellor."

"That's right, I am."

"So..." I said sarcastically, "you were a plant, sent to watch over me. So all your friendliness, the online stuff, the movie invitation... all that meant nothing."

"Michael, will you please shut up and let me speak?"

"Oh, go on. I'll enjoy watching you get out of this one."

She shook her head and said, "Michael, I'm not a paid-up counsellor working for the magistrate. I'm... I'm like you, an offender. I was sentenced to have a P.O.O.C.H. three months ago. I found it hard at first. It was hellish... Well, you know that yourself."

I stared at her, my face burning. I said, "An offender?"

She nodded. "I adapted well to P.O.O.C.H, after the initial difficulty. It nearly drove me mad, but I persevered, applied myself to his training. And you know what? It felt good. It felt great to overcome my initial... hostility, and actually succeed with him." She shrugged. "Anyway, they were impressed at the magistrates and asked me if I'd consider doing a little one-to-one work with other offenders on P.O.O.C.H. parole. I said yes, and you're my first."

"Your first...?" I said like an idiot. "So you're an offender..." I shook my head. "What did you do?"

She sighed. "Well, I suppose if we're going to be honest with each other and talk about you and Pooch, I should be open with you about..."

I winced. I wasn't looking forward to this, to finding out what Maxine had done. I mean, in the eyes of many I was a criminal offender too... but I didn't consider myself one.

She looked me straight in the eye and said, "Michael, after my mum died I went off the rails. I couldn't cope. I started..." She stopped, staring down at her hands. She looked up and went on, "I'd always wanted nice clothes, dresses and things. But Mum... she never encouraged me to... Well, she was a Baptist, you see. And very strict. And then, when she died... I wanted all these nice dresses and blouses and... and I couldn't bring myself to actually *buy* them. I know, I know, it was stupid... It was as if I didn't want the sales assistants to think..." She went red and shook her head. "I mean, I'm not exactly a fashion model, am I, and I didn't want them to laugh. So... I stole some dresses and stuff." She shrugged. "And I was caught." She glanced across the room at Pooch. "And I was P.O.O.C.H.ed."

"And you found it hard, at first?"

"Hard isn't the word. You know how it is. I wasn't *free* any more." She laughed. "Which is exactly why I received the punishment, of course. That, and it was to teach me... responsibility, and a bunch of other things. It made me realise that I wasn't the centre of the universe. I had to care for the needs of Sandy, and I came to realise that it wasn't all give on my part. After a while, I received something from him."

I stared at her and shook my head. "What was that?"

She looked down at her fingers again. "Affection, Michael. I'd... I'd never had that. Mum wasn't... she didn't show me much in the way of, you know, love. And I... I never had anyone. But Sandy... you must think I'm pathetic... but he gave me something, companionship, affection. I know, he wasn't a real dog. He was a robot. But even so..."

I smiled. "But even so, he's just like a real dog. Just as frustrating, and aggravating and..."

"And loving," she said. "And I miss him."

"Ah," I said. "You've come to the end of your sentence?"

She nodded. "I never thought I'd miss him, Michael. But I do."

I stared at the carpet between us, then I asked, "Would you like a cup of tea?"

"I'd love one."

While I made the tea I thought over what she'd said. I handed her the cup and asked, "When were you put on my case? Right at the start? Back when I was assigned Pooch, and –?"

"No. No, Michael. It was pure coincidence that we went to the same class, and played the same games... and had so much in common. And when I was asked to counsel you... I told them I knew you but they said that wasn't a problem. So I took the 'case'."

"I suppose I should tell you why I was assigned Pooch," I said.

She shook her head. "That doesn't matter, Michael. It's not why I'm here."

"You were honest with me. I'd feel better if you realised I wasn't a... real criminal."

"You mean, like me?"

I reddened. "I didn't mean it like that. Stealing a few dresses... that's not really criminal. Anyway, I hacked into a few banks accounts and..."

I told her my crime, and at the end of the confession she said, "But that's hardly a crime at all, Michael! I mean, some people would praise you for what you did."

I shrugged. "I was foolish to think I could change anything. And I did what I did not out of any altruism, I've come to realise, but out of a sense of impotence and frustration." I stared across at Pooch, who was curled up on the rug. "And I was punished with the hound from Hell."

Maxine sipped her tea and regarded me over the rim.

"What I came to realise," Maxine said, "is that when we feel anger towards our dogs – it's displaced anger. We're not really directing it at them, but at ourselves. And it's corrosive. We feel bad afterwards."

"I know. That's exactly how I feel, felt..."

"What you must understand, Michael, is that anger is futile. It serves absolutely no good. You feel it towards your dog because he's doing things that to him seem perfectly natural, but which don't fit in with your desires or your view of rationality. But you're really feeling anger towards yourself because deep down you're acknowledging your own ignorance and intolerance. When you come to realise this, and accept it, and see your dog as a wholly different being with needs and desires of his own, entirely different to yours, then you can do something to curb the anger and negative emotions you feel, towards him and towards yourself."

We sat in silence for a long time.

At last I looked up and said, "And how do I manage that?"

She smiled. "You live by the hour. You accept that Pooch has needs of his own. You accommodate his needs to your routine, and adapt the latter. Your anger will lessen, along with your frustration, and then you might come to accept that Pooch can show you affection."

"All very well in theory..." I said.

"Come on, Michael, let's go for a walk." She stood. "C'mon, Pooch."

Maxine popped round once a week for the next month and we chatted about how I was getting on.

I read dog training manuals and watched the DVD over and over. I worked to curb my anger. I tried not to see Pooch as an imposition on my lifestyle, but as an addition. Maxine made me realise the benefits of having the dog, benefits which in my frustration and ignorance I'd been unable to see.

"You've lost a lot of weight since the first time I've seen you, Michael. And you must be feeling fitter."

"True," I said.

"And you're leading a healthier life. Not eating as much rubbish."

"Pooch won't let me spend an hour in the greasy spoon... and I realised that what I was eating wasn't satisfying my hunger. I started eating a bit more fruit and veg."

"And your work and hobbies?"

I shrugged. "What about them?"

She smiled. "It's strange, but I found that to begin with I resented Sandy for taking me away from the things I liked doing. I make jewellery part-time, and I wasn't able to do as much – or so I thought at the time. I just had to learn to fit my work around him. The same with my painting. And do you know something? I came to feel that the time I spent jewellery-making and painting was *earned*, and I enjoyed it far more because of this. I just wondered if you felt the same."

I thought about it, then admitted, "Do you know something, I think you're right. When Pooch settles down, and I'm working on the web design..." I smiled. "I think I am bringing more to it. It's as if I appreciate my time far more, because, as you say, it's earned."

I was just beginning to enjoy my weekly sessions with Maxine when they ended. The counselling had run its course and she could report back that Michael Rice was responding satisfactorily and no longer exhibited violent tendencies towards his charge.

At our very last session, as we were about to part, Maxine paused in the hall and said, "I was wondering, Michael, as the sessions are over... I thought, I don't know, I mean... Well, perhaps it might be nice if we could meet up from time to time? And not just at the obedience classes..."

I looked away, stared at the peeling wallpaper and mumbled, "Well... er... why not?"

She smiled. "How about coffee on Friday, around the corner at Costa's? Say ten?"

"I'll be there. And so will Pooch."

It was strange, but I was terribly nervous that Friday as I met Maxine for a coffee. There was no longer the supportive context of my counselling as an excuse for our meeting, and I felt... *embarrassed.* The odd thing was that I think Maxine felt the same.

We chatted about dogs, at first, as if to break the ice – and then moved on to the latest games and movies. I almost asked her if she wanted to see the Forbidden Planet remake, but something stopped me.

A few days later I received an email from Maxine. "Terribly sorry, Michael. I have to go away for a month. A client in Devon needs counselling. We could meet up when I get back?"

The strange thing was that I felt both relief and at the same time disappointment, neither of which I could explain to myself.

Meanwhile, I came to see Pooch no longer as a ball and chain around my life. There were still times when his antics enraged me, but on these occasions I counted to ten and worked to calm myself, recalled Maxine's wise words, and those of the instructor on the DVD, and the moments of anger and frustration passed.

A month after Maxine went to Devon, I received an email from her. "Back to civilisation! I really missed London and my routine. How about a coffee later in the week?"

I held off replying. I considered my life, my own routine. In two weeks my sentence would come to an end and Pooch would be returned to the judiciary – and while a part of me did want to see

Maxine again... there was another part of me which wondered, with fear and trepidation, where my acceptance of her invitation might lead.

I told myself that I would consider replying tomorrow, and then *tomorrow*... and in consequence the days elapsed.

I missed the final obedience session, and then the day came when Pooch was taken away.

The doorbell chimed and a man stood on the threshold, his white van idling in the street.

I clipped Pooch's lead to his collar and led him from the bed-sit. At the door Pooch turned and stared up at me. Then he jumped up and lodged his massive paws on my shoulder. He looked into my eyes, something almost soulful in his expression.

You're nothing but a machine, I told myself.

"Goodbye, Pooch," I said.

The man took the lead. "Expect you'll be glad to see the back of him, hm?"

"You bet," I said.

He led Pooch down the path and into the back of the van. Pooch stared out at me from his crate, and I watched as the van moved off down the road and turned the corner.

*Just a machine*, I told myself.

I tried to relish my freedom, to slip back into the carefree pre-Pooch days. I thought I'd lie in, but found myself getting up at six as if I had a dog to walk; I thought I'd fill the time I normally walked the dog with work – but found myself taking a stroll around the park just the same.

And then, when I was working, I'd look up and across the room to where Pooch had taken to lying on the old sofa, and with a start I'd realise he was no longer there.

I fully intended to get in touch with Maxine again, but as the weeks passed I found it hard to contact her and explain my incommunicado.

Then one day I was strolling through the park when I saw a familiar figure coming towards me. "Oh, hi," I said.

She smiled, but without recognising me.

"Michael Rice," I said. "You represented me six months ago little over. I was P.O.O.C.H.ed."

She looked me up and down, and then said, "Mr Rice, of course. But my, you've changed. I hardly recognised you."

I just shrugged.

She went on, "And are you getting out these days, Mr Rice, and meeting people?"

I stammered something and hurried off.

That afternoon as I was eating a sandwich at my desk and considering the encounter, I turned and said something to the absent dog. Five minutes later I realised what I had to do.

I made a phone call.

Then I sat down before my PC and composed an email in my head.

Sweating, I tapped 'Maxine' into the address, took a breath and began:

Maxine! I'm so sorry for not getting in touch. I was busy... a web-design job came along. I should have contacted you, but... I was wondering if we could meet up for a coffee in the morning.

I pressed *send* and waited. And waited.

An hour later a message appeared in my inbox.

Michael, she wrote, great to hear from you. I've been busy too. Would love a coffee. How are you getting on without Pooch? See you at Costa's at ten!

"So, Michael, tell me about the web design job you've been so busy with?"

I shrugged uncomfortably, wondering if she could see through my lie. "Oh, it was nothing special, but a long job... How are you getting on without Sandy?" I asked, changing the subject. "Do you still miss him?"

Maxine nodded. "I miss him terribly." She looked at me. "You?" she asked. "Do you miss Pooch?"

"That's one of the reasons I wanted to see you this morning," I said. "I want your help, and advice. I wonder if you'd come somewhere with me."

"Intriguing. Where?"

I told her.

Maxine beamed at me. "Let's do that," she said.

I stood up and left the coffee shop, then stopped dead. "Oh, *shit*,"

I said. I lifted my foot and stared down at the mess plastered across the sole.

Maxine laughed. "Well, they do say it's lucky, Michael."

"They do, don't they?" I said, and couldn't stop myself from laughing along with her as we strolled south towards Battersea Dogs' Home.

# About the Author

Eric Brown began writing when he was fifteen, while living in Australia, and sold his first short story to Interzone in 1986. He has won the British Science Fiction Award twice for his short stories, has published over fifty books, and his work has been translated into sixteen languages. His latest books include the SF novels *The Serene Invasion*, *Satan's Reach*, and *Salvage*, and the crime novel *Murder by the Book*. He writes a regular science fiction review column for the Guardian newspaper and lives near Dunbar, East Lothian. His website can be found at: www.ericbrown.co.uk

# *Imaginings*

## The Way Ahead

A series of collections, each volume featuring the work of a single selected author, *Imaginings* brings together the very best of that author's uncollected short fiction plus pieces wholly original to the book.

Each volume is released as a signed and numbered hardback edition, strictly limited in number, plus an e-book version. There is no paperback edition.

The hardback editions are available to buy via the NewCon Press website, priced at between £19.99 and £22.99.

Or… *Imaginings* can be purchased via **subscription.** The advantages?

- Reduced price. Four volumes: £82.00, inclusive of shipping within the UK (reduced shipping costs if overseas).
- Subscribers 'buy' a number within the limited edition run, which remains theirs exclusively until subscription lapses, at which point it will become available to others.
- In addition to the numbered hardback, subscribers receive a free copy of the e-book (kindle and e-pub).
- Subscribers are guaranteed a copy of a very limited book likely to sell out rapidly and become highly collectable.

Volume 1, January 2012: Tanith Lee
Volume 2, April 2012: Stephen Baxter
Volume 3, September 2012: Tony Ballantyne
Volume 4, December 2012: Lisa Tuttle
Volume 5, April 2013: Nina Allan
Volume 6, August 2013: Adrian Tchaikovsky
Volume 7, November 2013: Steve Rasnic Tem
Volume 8, April 2014: Eric Brown